GARBAGE CREEK

and other stories by

W.D.VALGARDSON

WITH ILLUSTRATIONS BY

Michel Bisson

A GROUNDWOOD BOOK

DOUGLAS & McINTYRE

TORONTO VANCOUVER BERKELEY

Groundwood Books/Douglas & McIntyre Ltd.
720 Bathurst Street, Suite 500, Toronto, Ontario M5S 2R4

Distributed in the U.S.A. by Publishers Group West
1700 Fourth Street, Berkeley, CA 94710

We acknowledge the financial support of the Canada Council for
the Arts, the Ontario Arts Council and the Government of Canada
through the Book Publishing Industry Development Program for
our publishing activities.

ONTARIO ARTS COUNCIL
CONSEIL DES ARTS DE L'ONTARIO

Canadian Cataloguing in Publication Data
Valgardson, W.D.
Garbage creek, and other stories
"A Groundwood book."
ISBN 0-88899-339-0
I. Bisson, Michel. II. Title.
PS8593.A53G37 1998   jC813'.54   C97-930841-0
PZ7.V34Ga 1998

Design by Michael Solomon
Illustrations by Michel Bisson
Printed and bound in Canada by Webcom

To my granddaughter,
Rebecca Rae

TABLE OF CONTENTS

They were having breakfast when the phone rang. Erin's father answered it. It was one of his usual conversations.

"Yup, yup, nope, yup, nope, hmmm, maybe, yup, yup."

He hung up without saying good-bye. He never said good-bye. He thought saying good-bye was a waste of time.

"They know you've gone good-bye," he always said, "because you've hung up."

He went back to eating his porridge.

"Well?" Erin said. Sometimes her friends called and her father forgot to tell her. Once a conversation was over, it was over. Getting him to remember that there had been a message took a little doing. Especially at harvest time or calving time when he started work before dawn and kept working until after dark.

"Good porridge," he said, putting more brown sugar on it.

"Any message?" Erin asked. "Like a meteor hit the school? The bus drivers are on strike? It's going to hail?"

"No hail," her father replied, the spoon stopping halfway to his mouth. The word hail always got his attention. Hail destroyed the barley and canola and flax. "Some city guy wants to buy that forty acres of scrub in the southeast corner."

Erin laughed. "Nobody can farm there. That's swamp and rock."

"Doesn't want to farm. Wants to build a cottage."

"Mom," Erin said, after her father had left. "We wouldn't sell those forty acres, would we?" That was her favorite part of their land. The rest of the two sections they owned had all been cleared. The trees had been cut down, hauled into piles and set on fire. The canola was beautiful when it bloomed. A sea of yellow. The flax was an endless lake of soft blue. But after the harvest, there was just bare ground.

Erin went out to feed the chickens. Her father was gassing up the tractor.

"You wouldn't really sell those forty acres, would you?" she asked.

"Not much good for anything. As you said, it's just rock and swamp. Not even any good-sized trees for lumber. If something's not paying its way, you've got to let it go."

As Erin scattered the grain, she thought about how her mom had said it cost a fortune to keep her in clothes. And then there was the food she ate. And her piano lessons. And her books for school. And. And. And. She wasn't paying her way. Even though she fed the chickens and helped weed the garden.

She wished her dad was easier to talk to. She loved him a lot, but it was hard to have a conversation when he mostly talked one word at a time. The words he used most were yup and nope. He said he didn't believe much in conversation. Erin, on the other hand, loved to talk. She could talk about any thing, any time, any where. Her mom liked to talk, too.

Her dad said with two women in the house who liked to talk, it was lucky he was such a good listener. Except Erin sometimes had to say, "You forgot your hat," three times before he heard her.

As she waited for the school bus, she studied the forty acres. She loved those forty acres. She played there a lot. She knew all the paths. She'd hoped some day to buy them from her father and mother so she could have her own place.

On the way to school, she ignored the boys throwing each other's caps around.

"What's the matter?" Tessa asked. Tessa was her best friend.

"Nothing," Erin said. "I've just gotta think."

She thought all the way through math and science and recess. In English class, they were supposed to write a story. Ms. James, their teacher, said, "Write what you know about. Write what you care about. Show, don't tell. That's the way to get people to pay attention to you."

"Show, don't tell," Erin thought. "Show, don't tell." It stuck in her head.

When she went to bed that night, the last thing she thought about was Ms. James saying, "Show, don't tell."

"I don't want you to sell those forty acres," Erin said at breakfast.

"Yup," her dad said.

"Does that mean you won't?"

"Nope."

"But I love it."

"If you can't grow grain on it, what good is it?"

It was Saturday. Erin's mother and father went to harvest, her dad driving the tractor and her mom the truck. Erin walked over to the forty acres.

"Not good for anything," she thought as she looked around. She wished she didn't have to wear a brace on her leg. Not good for anything was the way some people felt about her. Because she couldn't run fast, they didn't want her on their baseball team. She couldn't play soccer or go skating. Just keeping up when everybody was walking fast was difficult.

The doctor said some day she'd be able to go without the brace. But he'd been saying that for a long time now.

There were hazelnut bushes growing like a hedge along one side of low ground. Erin pushed two of the bushes apart. There were hazelnuts in their fuzzy brown jackets. The jackets had started to split so she knew they were ready. She had to be careful so the prickles didn't stick in her fingers. She used her nails to pull the jacket apart and take out the nut. She found a rock and cracked the hard shell. The nut was soft and sweet. She went back to the house and got a bag. Then she returned and began picking hazelnuts. She picked until the bag was full. When she got back to the house, she filled up a bowl and put it in her room.

Then she went back with a basket. The year before, she'd seen high-bush cranberries. Cranberry jelly was her father's favorite.

Erin followed the rabbit paths that wound through the bush.

She didn't find any high-bush cranberries, but she did find chokecherries. She ran her hand down a stem. The berries filled her hand. She put them in her mouth. The juice was sweet but it made her mouth and throat feel dry. She loved the taste.

"Chokecherry jelly," she said to her mom when she came in for lunch. "There's lots and lots of chokecherries." She spread her arms wide to show how many.

"We haven't got time right now," her mother said, glancing at the sky. At this time of year, they were always afraid of rain or hail or snow. They had to get the crop off the land. Her father didn't even stop to eat. Her mom just made sandwiches and tea for him and handed them up into the tractor. He ate as he bumped along.

"I can do it," Erin replied. She got out the colander and washed the berries in it. Then she put them in the jelly pot with its thick bottom that kept the berries from scorching. She put the pot on the stove and turned on the ring.

"You've got to crush some with a fork," her mother said.

"Got to get the juice started," Erin replied. "I know that."

Erin cooked the berries, then searched in the cupboard for the jelly bag. After the juice and skins and seeds had cooled, she poured the mess out into the jelly bag. Then she tied the bag to the back of a wooden chair. She already had a large bowl underneath the bag. The bowl was to collect the juice.

After lunch, Erin went back out to her forty acres. She was determined to find high-bush cranberries. These weren't the kind you could buy in the store. Those berries grew low in the swamp. The prairie kind grew in large red clumps on small trees.

As she was walking quietly along the path, she saw something move in a grove of spruce. She stopped. She tried to see what was there in the shadows. She could feel her heart beating faster. From time to time, bears came south when there wasn't enough for them to eat. Erin didn't want to see one close up. They had big teeth and big claws and her dad said they looked on young girls as tasty snacks. With her brace on, she couldn't run very fast.

She stood absolutely still. The wind was coming toward her so whatever was in front of her wouldn't have smelled her. Something moved in the shadows. Erin leaned forward without moving her feet. She didn't want to step on anything that would make a noise.

Just then a deer stepped into a patch of sunlight. It was a buck with three-pronged antlers. Just behind him came a doe.

The two deer walked back into the shadows. Erin could hear them moving away. If they were going to cross the highway, she hoped that they'd do it when no cars were coming.

"Been exploring?" her dad said when she arrived back at the house. He was refueling.

"Yup," she said.

"Seen any deer?"

She held up two fingers. That's what he was always doing to her.

"You'd think he couldn't talk and had to use hand signals," she said to her mother as they poured the juice from the chokecherries into the pot.

"He's a good listener," her mother said. "There aren't a lot of good listeners around, so you learn to appreciate them."

Erin added sugar and some crabapples. The crabapples were to make the jelly thicken.

"I didn't know you knew so much about making jelly," her mother said.

"I've been watching. And I helped you the year before last. How come we never made jelly last year?"

"No time," her mother said. She was already heading out the door. "I think a couple of the chickens got out of their pen. Could you catch them and put them back in?"

Chickens! Erin hated chickens. They were the dumbest creatures on earth. They were so dumb that if you tucked their heads under their wings, they thought it was night and fell asleep. They didn't even know enough to take their heads out and look around. That was her father's favorite thing to say when someone did something really dumb. "Dumber than a chicken."

She didn't want to chase chickens. But she knew she had to. If she didn't, they'd wander onto the road and get run over by a car. She wished they'd all get run over. It was because of them that the kids had started to call her the Chicken Lady. Her mom had the idea that Erin could earn some money of her own by taking fresh eggs to school and selling them to the teachers. Right away Tommy Robbins started hooting and hollering and shouting, "Here comes the Chicken Lady."

He didn't stop teasing her until she found an egg that had gone bad and put it in his boot. When he pulled on his boot and broke the egg, the smell was so bad they nearly had to evacuate the school. Tommy had to go home and get clean socks and clean shoes. Erin got a detention and her dad had to come and pick her up. After that she said she was never selling eggs again, not for anybody, not for anything.

Erin herded the chickens back into the pen and made sure the gate was shut. Then she got her camera and went back to her forty acres. She crept along the trail, looking for the deer. When she got to the spruce grove, she couldn't see anything. She knew they might be sleeping.

While she was waiting, a bush rabbit came hopping along the trail. When it was close, she whistled sharply. The rabbit stopped and stood on its hind legs. Erin took its picture. When it heard the click of the camera, it scampered away.

She crept closer to the spruce trees, peering into the shadows, hoping that the deer would stand up and walk into the sunlight. When she got close, she saw that they were gone. There was just the packed-down grass where they had bedded down.

She started to follow their trail. The hoofprints led her to a small clearing where there'd been a fire the year before. While she was searching for hoofprints, she saw a morel. Morels were a kind of mushroom that looked like little brown Christmas trees. She remembered searching for them with her dad. He said they grew in places where there'd been a fire. She found one, then another, and another. She filled her bag. Morels were very special. The first Ukrainians who had settled in the area had picked them. There was even a large sculpture of a morel in a little park on the highway.

When Erin got back to the house, she got a needle and thread and strung the morels on the thread. Then she hung the strings around her room.

At church the next morning, the minister gave a sermon on miracles. Erin didn't believe in miracles. If there were miracles, someone would have been able to fix her leg so she didn't have to wear a brace all the time. Then she could play soccer and go skating with the other kids.

After the service she heard her mother and a friend discussing Erin's dad.

"It would take a miracle to change his mind once it's made up," her mother said.

"Amen," Erin said out loud. Her mother gave her That Look.

When they got home, Erin took her camera and went back to her forty acres. The deer hadn't come back, so she collected some red and yellow leaves. She searched for flowers, but most had stopped blooming for the year.

At school the next day, she went to the library and made copies of pictures of the Indian paintbrush and lady slipper. The pink and yellow lady slippers were, the book said, northern orchids.

"Orchids," she said to Tessa. "I didn't think orchids grew this far north."

After school, she discovered a wild plum tree and picked a bucket of plums. There was no time to go looking for anything on Tuesday or Wednesday. On Thursday, she looked again for the deer. On Friday, she had drama club after school.

The phone call came while they were having pancakes Saturday morning.

"Yup," her father said. "Yup, yup, nope, yup. Okay."

"Any message for me?" Erin asked before her father had a chance to forget what he'd talked about. He was already listening to the weather report.

"City people," he said. "They're going to come look at the property tomorrow."

"Tomorrow!" Erin said. Her voice sounded like barbed wire in the wind, high and whiny. "I thought they weren't interested in buying until next spring."

She went out to her forty acres. She sat down on her stump, the one where she always sat when things weren't going right. When Tessa didn't want to be her best friend any more, when Tommy Robbins called her the Chicken Lady, when she wanted to go ice skating and could only stand at the side of the rink and watch.

She'd made a lot of friends here at her stump. There were the orioles that had a long nest that looked like a sack, and the crows that nested at the top of a spruce tree. There were the rabbits she was always bumping into and the deer that mysteriously slipped in and out of the bush. There was the creek in which the carp and jackfish came up to spawn in the spring. The creek was so shallow that she was able to squat at the edge of the water and watch their every move. In spring there were all the bushes in bloom and, underfoot, patches of marsh marigolds. Sometimes she caught tadpoles and even frogs.

Erin thought about Ms. James again. "Show, don't tell." She got up and went to the far corner of the property. There she finally found not one but three high-bush cranberry bushes loaded with the large heads of red berries. They were easy to pick. The heads were bigger than her two hands. But it was too late. There wasn't time to make jelly and put it in jars with nice labels. That would take a couple of days.

"Sometimes you've just got to let things go," her dad had said when their dog Jameson was run over by a grain truck. "He can't be fixed." That was the closest her dad had ever come to making a speech.

Erin picked one of the heads of berries and took it back to the house.

The next morning before anyone else was up, Erin lined up the jars of chokecherry jelly on the cupboard. She lay the bright-red heads of cranberries beside the jars. She strung up the drying morels. She pasted the brightly colored leaves onto a large sheet of paper and wrote the names of the trees under them. She put up pictures of the butterflies that lived in the bush, along with her snapshot of the rabbit.

She'd pressed some flowers that spring. She put those up beside the pictures she'd got at the library. The deer hadn't come back so she didn't have a photograph. Instead, she pasted up a picture of a buck and doe and a fawn that she'd cut out of a magazine.

She lettered a long strip of paper that said, "This is our home. Don't take it away." Her dad had said he'd be happy to get twenty-five hundred dollars for the forty acres. She took the twenty-seven dollars and thirty-five cents that she'd saved and put it on the cupboard with an IOU for two thousand four hundred and seventy-two dollars and sixty-five cents and a note saying that she'd start selling eggs again.

Then she went outside. She'd done her best but she knew there wasn't any point. Her dad wouldn't get it. She went back to her stump and was still sitting there when a car she didn't recognize pulled up and a couple got out. Her dad shook hands with them and then they went for a walk around the property. The woman had high-heeled shoes that kept getting stuck and coming off.

After awhile, they reappeared. Erin's dad walked them to the car. They stood there for quite awhile. The man was talking a lot. She could see her dad saying yup. He must have said yup about ten thousand times. Sometimes he said nope. She knew that because when he said nope he always shook his head. Her dad and the man shook hands and the man gave her dad a piece of paper. It looked like a check. Then the couple drove away.

Erin stayed on her stump for an hour. Then she decided that she just had to adjust to some things whether she liked it or not. Like Jameson getting run over. Like having to wear a brace. Like having a dad with a six-word vocabulary.

Even though it was Sunday, her parents had started harvesting again. There were some clouds in the sky and they were in a hurry to get the crop in. When she got to the yard, a chicken had got loose again.

"Stupid chicken," she yelled and herded it back into the pen.

When she went inside, she started to put away the jelly and the mushrooms and her pictures. Then she saw that someone had put a picture of her in the middle of the display.

When she looked on the cupboard, she saw that the twenty-seven dollars and thirty-five cents and the IOU were gone. In their place was a contract. It was in her dad's handwriting. It said, "Forty acres sold to Erin for two thousand five hundred dollars. No interest."

There was a piece of paper on the cupboard. It looked like the piece of paper the man had given her father. Erin picked it up. She turned it over. It wasn't a check. It was just a name and a phone number.

Suddenly Erin realized she'd better go out and make friends with the chickens. They were going to have to lay a lot of eggs.

CYBERSPACE SAM

Solitario Adolphus Muggins surfed the Net, read CD-ROMs, e-mailed and down-loaded more than was good for him. Or so his family thought.

After breakfast one Saturday, his mother asked the family where they were going.

"To the mall to be with my friends," Carol said.

"To the schoolyard to shoot some baskets," his

brother, Greg, said. He was home from college for the summer.

"To the garage to get a tire repaired," his father said.

They all turned to look at Solitario Adolphus Muggins, or Sam, as they called him.

"Cyberspace," he replied.

"That kid's got a problem," his brother said, after Sam had disappeared into the Internet.

"It's just a stage," his mother said. "With you it was skateboards."

"He reads the dictionary," his sister complained. "If we don't do something, he'll carry a briefcase and wear one of those plastic things in his shirt pocket when he goes into grade nine. I'll be ostracized."

"We need to open a dialogue with him," his father said. He taught at the local college. "Communication is everything."

At supper, Sam's father suddenly blurted out, "Dinosaurs." Someone at work had told him dinosaurs were very popular.

"A group of extinct reptiles, widely distributed during the Mesozoic period. Anything you want to know, I can find for you on http://cord.iupui.edu /~nmrosentallabout.html." To mark the slashes, Sam swung his right hand up and down at an angle.

"What am I going to do?" Carol asked her mother. "His role model is Data. He wants to be an android."

Their mother's basic life philosophy was that everything would come out all right eventually, but even she looked a bit concerned. Sort of the way she'd looked when Carol had got her nose ring.

"I was transplanting baby's breath today and as he went by he said, 'Gypsophila,' just like that."

"You see what I mean?" Carol said. "Weird."

The next morning, Carol, who really loved her brother dearly, stopped beside Sam. "Hit EXIT!" she ordered. When the screen-saver came on, she put her hand on his shoulder. "You need to get a life."

"I live everywhere," Sam answered. "I have e-mail from thirty-six countries."

"You're twelve," his sister said. "And I'll bet you don't even know the difference between boys and girls."

"Don't be ridiculous. Of course I do. Girls have two X chromosomes. Boys have an X and a Y."

When Carol told her father about this incident, he agreed that something drastic had to be done.

"All his reality is virtual," Greg said. "We've got to get him in touch with real reality. Here and now."

But what, they all asked each other. What and where and how would there be no computer, no batteries, no disks, no programs, no e-mail, no cyberspace, no Internet, no Web.

"Camping," Sam's father shouted, snapping his fingers.

"Camping," Greg shouted back.

"Camping," Carol agreed with a sigh. She didn't like camping, but she was desperate. When he got to high school, Sam would be a bigger liability than a pair of Nikes among the Doc Martens.

"I can't go," Sam's mother said. "I've got reports to write." She attended meetings for the Social Services ministry. "I'll drop you off and pick you up in two days at the provincial park."

They sang "One Hundred Bottles of Beer on the Wall" all the way to the starting point. That is, Sam's father and mother and brother and sister sang. Sam played computer games on a pad of paper. He knew the opening situations by heart.

"Look at your brother," his father said when they were setting up camp. "Getting the canoes packed for tomorrow. That's experience working. Practice makes perfect. Look at your sister chopping wood. That's the result of lifting those weights. And watch me whip together supper over an open fire." He took a deep breath. "There's nothing like it. The Great Outdoors. Just like our ancestors."

"In Finland, people have saunas," Sam said. "You heat rocks until they're red-hot, then pour water over them. You get hot as a roasting ham, then run outside and roll around in the snow. That's what ago.helsinki.pi tells me. He says that's what makes men, men. Personally, I like lukewarm showers and a warm bath towel."

"Wait until tomorrow when we get into our canoes and start down the river. You'll forget all this computer stuff for a couple of days. We'll be coureurs de bois." His father tried to sing something in French but he couldn't remember the words, so he sang a couple of verses of Davy Crockett with a French accent.

That night Sam lay awake, staring at the stars.

"Beautiful," Carol sighed. "I wonder what their names are?"

"If you'd have let me bring my laptop, I could have told you. I have a star identification program."

"You're hopeless," she snapped. "Go to sleep."

The next morning, they headed out in two canoes. Greg and Carol were in one, and Sam and his father were in the other. They had all their equipment in the center of the canoes. The river was fast but shallow. In some places, they had to jump out and drag the canoes over the gravel bottom. Sometimes there were pools. They stopped and swam in these and had water fights.

They had lunch on a sandbar. They stopped to do some fishing and caught two fish, which they put in a cooler so they could have them for supper.

"This is reality, see," Greg explained. "Everything's

in real time. You've got to grunt and sweat to get somewhere. No make-believe. This is where you learn to deal with life." Greg always wore white socks and played six different sports.

"Here, and in the mall. Social life is real, too. You've got to learn to get along, Sam. Fit in. Manners make the man," Carol added.

"There's manners on the Internet," Sam replied. "You don't follow them, you get flamed."

"If you're going to be weird, keep it in," Greg said. "Deal with reality."

They canoed with the current, guiding the canoes around rocks and trees and sandbars. They saw deer and raccoons and lots of birds.

The current picked up speed. They were coming around a sharp curve when Sam's canoe swung to the side, hit a fallen tree and tipped sideways with the open part toward the current. Sam jumped clear, but his father fell on his side and his right leg went under the canoe. The canoe pinned him to the gravel bottom. Then the force of the water pushed him and the canoe under the tree trunk. Sam's father tried to pull free but the weight of the canoe held him against the bottom.

Greg and Carol jumped out of their canoe. They grabbed the tipped-over canoe and pulled on it with all their might. The force of the water was too great. The canoe kept edging farther under the tree.

With each inch, Sam's father was forced down into the water. He had to push himself up to keep his head from going under.

"Grab one end," Greg yelled. All three of them grabbed one end and tried to pivot the canoe. The canoe twisted slightly but pulled their father farther under.

"Pull!" Sam's father yelled. "It'll drag me down."

They pulled and pushed with all their might. The canoe moved under again.

"Help," Carol called, but there wasn't anyone around. There were just some cows in a nearby field watching them curiously.

"Help!" Greg called. Nobody heard him.

The canoe held steady. Then a rock that was blocking it pulled loose, and the canoe scraped forward. Their father's head was nearly pulled under water.

Sam yelled, "X equals s times r." He let go of the canoe.

"What are you doing?" Greg yelled back.

"X equals s times r," Sam repeated. He scrambled around in the water on his hands and knees.

"Help," Greg and Carol both yelled. They were straining with all their might but the canoe was pulling them forward.

Sam ignored them. He stood up suddenly, holding the ax that had fallen out of the canoe.

"Not my leg," his father yelled. "Don't chop off my leg!"

Sam ran around to the back of the canoe and took a swing. He chopped a hole in the canoe, then another one, and another one. He kept chopping, making more and more holes.

"Are you crazy?" his brother screamed. "What'll we tell the rental people?"

"X equals s times r," Sam shouted back.

He kept chopping until there was a long line of holes. His brother and sister pulled with all their might, and the canoe gradually lifted off the bottom. His father dragged his leg from underneath.

They helped him to shore. They set up the tent, rescued the rest of the equipment and dragged the two canoes up onto the bank.

"What were you yelling?" his father asked. His leg wasn't broken, but it looked like an overripe banana in places.

"The formula for water pressure against a surface. The force equals the surface times the rate of the current. We needed to create more pressure than that to free the canoe. We couldn't do it. So we had two alternatives. Stop the water. We couldn't do that. Or reduce the size of the surface. I reduced the size of the surface. There's sort of a Web site for physics. We work out problems and stuff."

Greg and Carol looked at each other. Then they

stared at Sam but didn't say anything. Their father patted Sam on the head.

"We'll stay here tonight," he said. "Then you'll have to walk along beside the good canoe and float me down to the park. I'm not going to be walking for a couple of days."

"If I had a cellular," Sam said, "we'd be out of here in no time."

THE SECRET

Johnny and Marianne lived at the end of the road on the shore of Lake Winnipeg. Their father was a commercial fisherman. The nearest town was more than thirty miles away. The road that led through the forest and swamps and ended just past their camp was often unusable. In winter, snow drifts stretched across it. In spring and fall, water flooded it.

One afternoon as they were picking saskatoonberries along the lake shore, Marianne said, "Listen." She raised her hand and cocked her head to one side.

Johnny froze in place. He could hear the small sighing sound of the waves lapping on the beach. There was the distant sound of an outboard motor.

"I don't hear anything," he said. He wanted to get back to picking berries. Their mother had promised them she would take the berries into town and sell them to the storekeeper. Johnny had his heart set on buying a pair of ice skates that he'd seen in the catalog. Shiny black ones with new laces to replace the old pair that he had to tie up with seaming twine from his father's nets. The skates were so old that the leather had faded to a pale brown, and the toes were as fuzzy as the brown husk of a hazelnut.

Marianne wanted a blue jacket with a fringe along the arms.

"Ssshhh!" Marianne held her finger to her lips. "Hear it? It sounds like someone crying."

They crouched there, listening. Just then, for a moment, something whimpered.

"Let's go see what it is," Marianne said.

"We're supposed to stay on the beach. There was a bear prowling around last night."

"We'll just go a little ways," Marianne said. "Just so we can hear where it's coming from. What if someone's lost?"

Reluctantly, Johnny took a long stick from a driftwood pile. His sister was a year older than him. Every time Marianne said just, they ended up getting into trouble. Let's just see if we can row the boat to the point. Let's just see if we can catch a baby skunk. They'd both had to sleep outside in a tent after that adventure.

He looked at his basket. "It's only half full," he complained.

The forest was cool and full of shadows. There was only a thin layer of soil. Beneath that was white limestone that had formed when the whole area had been a great lake. Here and there the limestone had cracked and collapsed. There were deep crevices and holes. In some places, fallen branches and leaves and moss covered the crevices.

Johnny and Marianne were constantly warned not to play in this area. Anyone stepping in the wrong spot could tumble down and be trapped at the bottom.

Johnny probed the ground with the stick. Marianne walked directly behind him. Hardly any light sifted down through the trees.

Johnny probed, testing the ground, then moved ahead. He stopped and probed again. Each time they stopped, they turned their heads this way and that, listening. It was so quiet they could hear their own hearts beating.

Then, all at once, they heard a sharp whine, as if someone was in pain.

"Over there," Marianne whispered, pointing to her right.

Johnny kept probing with his stick, making sure the ground was solid. He carefully pushed away the branches.

His stick broke through the surface.

"Stop," he whispered. He knocked away the covering of leaves and moss. In front of them was a deep, dark crevice. "It's too wide to cross. We'll have to follow along until it narrows."

A branch cracked. They both stopped. They turned their heads from side to side. Johnny made the word "Bear?" with his mouth but made no noise. Marianne shook her head. They waited, ready to run back to the beach. The forest was full of unexpected noises—trees rubbing branches, deer or moose feeding, birds hopping about on the ground searching for food.

When there was no more cracking, the kind of cracking made by a bear walking on dry twigs, they edged along the crevice until it was narrow enough to cross. But they lost the direction from which the sound had come.

One of the things they'd learned from going hunting with their father was to wait patiently and silently, sometimes for an hour. When they made noise, the animals hid and were silent. When they were silent, the animals started moving around and making noise.

After they had waited without moving for ten minutes, they were rewarded with the sound of a whimper.

"Back this way," Marianne motioned.

They crawled under a tree that had blown down. They pushed aside cranberry and hazel bushes. Moose maple blocked their way.

"I don't think we should go in there," Johnny said. Because the trees were so close, it was as dark as early evening. "Let's go back." He was thinking about all the saskatoonberries that were waiting to be picked.

Even as he quietly said it, Marianne was pushing her way through the brush.

"Stop!" he said and caught the back of Marianne's shirt. She was teetering on the edge of a narrow crevice.

All at once, there were three sharp barks. They both stared into the shadows of the crevice.

"Look!" Marianne said.

At the bottom of the crevice, staring up at them, was a wolf pup. He was gray and had a streak of white just above one ear.

"I'll tell Dad. He can bring a gun and shoot it."

"No!" Marianne cried. "It's just a baby."

The wolf pup had seen them. It yipped defiant-ly, then backed up into a crack so all they could see were its green eyes and the tip of its nose. It kept one paw off the ground.

"It's hurt its leg," Johnny said nervously. "We'd better tell someone."

"No," Marianne said, catching his arm. "This is our secret. They'll kill it. I'll bet it was the mother that was hit by a car last week. Someone said there was a pup with it."

"We can't leave it here. It'll starve to death."

Marianne emptied her basket of berries into the crevice.

"What are you doing?" Johnny demanded. "Those are to pay for your jacket."

"They're my berries," Marianne replied defiantly. "I can do what I want with them."

Johnny didn't talk to Marianne for the rest of the afternoon. They picked berries in silence. Just before they went in to have supper, she made him promise to not tell anyone about the pup.

That evening, after he'd gone to bed, Marianne came to see him. "I'm going to take care of him. If you won't help, I'll do it myself."

"You don't even know if it's a him. Maybe it's a her."

"It doesn't matter." She got that look she always got when she thought he was being dumb. Her eyebrows got closer together and she looked at him from under her eyelids.

"Wolves eat deer," Johnny whispered back.

"People eat deer," Marianne replied.

"Wolves eat people."

"How many people do you know who've killed wolves?"

"Dad, Uncle Ben, Old Joe, lots of people."

"And how many wolves do you know who've killed people?"

He thought about it for a minute. "None," he admitted.

The next day they went to the gut pile. Every morning, before the sun was up, their father went out on the lake and lifted his nets. Every noon he came home and unloaded his fish. After lunch he cleaned the fish. Then Johnny and Marianne took the heads and guts into a clearing in the forest and dumped them. The smell, especially in the warm weather, was terrible.

"Worse than a skunk," Johnny said. "I'd rather be sprayed by a skunk than fall into a gut pile."

"Be quiet," Marianne replied. "This is for Gunnar."

"Gunnar? Who's Gunnar?" He stared at her. He tried to think the way that she would think, but it was difficult. Suddenly, he got it. "You can't give him a name. Wolves don't have names."

"Gunnar," she said, "was a brave hero. He fought against big odds."

Marianne took a plastic bread bag out of her pocket.

"Put this over your hand," she ordered.

"Why?" He was starting to get a sinking sensation in his stomach, sort of the way he felt when he ate too many cookies, then went out on the boat with his father and there were a lot of waves. He just knew he was going to puke.

Marianne pulled out a plastic shopping bag.

"Pick up some fish heads and put them in here," she said.

"Not me, no sir," Johnny said. "I'm not picking up fish guts. Not for anybody." He started making gagging sounds.

"You can have half the saskatoons I pick from now on," she said.

"Skates," he said to himself. "Brand-new, shiny skates." Then he held his breath and started picking up fish heads and putting them in the bag.

Every day after that, they carried a bag of fish heads and tails and dumped them into the crevice. Since Marianne was so determined and since he was going with her anyway, Johnny got a plastic bucket and a rope out of their father's storage shed. He filled it with water at the lakeshore and lowered it to the wolf pup. There were lots of mice around the fish camp. Johnny set traps for them.

"Wolves like mice," he said. "I read it in a book by that Farley Mowat guy."

"You're being really nice," Marianne said. "I'm glad you changed your mind."

"We can keep him until the winter comes. Then his fur will be prime," Johnny told Marianne. They had been picking berries every day and taken them to town to be sold. Johnny had his money in a glass sealer beside his bed.

"No," Marianne shouted angrily. "There's more important things than money. That's all you think about. Jingle jangle." She imitated him shaking his money jar. Even with Marianne giving him half her berries, his jar wasn't filling up very fast. "Wolves have feelings. Just like you and me."

"Dumb animals," Johnny said.

"You said it," Marianne said. "Not me."

For a few days they avoided each other, but then Johnny asked Marianne to play catch with him. Playing catch by bouncing a ball off the side of the ice shed was no fun.

One day a fur buyer came by. He said he'd be interested in buying pelts that winter. "Good money for fur this year. You going to run a trap line? You're old enough now, Johnny. You got some furs, you could make yourself a little money."

A few weeks after that there was a skim of snow on the grass. At the lake the rocks had collars of clear ice. Soon the lake would be covered in ice all the way to the horizon.

Johnny hoped there'd be no wind for the next few weeks. All summer he'd imagined the day when the ice would be strong enough to hold him. It would be as clear as glass, without a mark on it, and then he'd sit on a rock and tie on his new skates. He'd stand up on the ice and glide over the surface. He'd have the biggest skating rink in the world. He'd skate during the day time. He'd skate at night under the moon.

After testing the ice he and Marianne went inside. Johnny emptied his money jar onto his bed. After he counted it, he said, "There's not enough here for skates." He had the page from the catalog tacked up over his bed. He took the picture down, crumpled it up and threw it on the floor.

He ran outside.

Marianne ran after him.

He was swallowed up by the forest but she knew where he'd be. She found him standing, staring into the crevice.

The wolf had grown over the last two months. He was stretched up on his hind legs, looking at them. His leg had healed. He gave three quick barks, whined and waited for them to throw him some fish.

Just then a wolf howled in the distance. The pup cocked his head as if he were asking them a question. He scrabbled at the stone wall as if he was trying to climb it, tipped his head back and howled in reply. He howled four times. He started to pace quickly back and forth, then made a short run and jumped. His feet caught at the stone but he slipped back.

"He wants to be free," Johnny said. He was thinking of what it would have been like to have had the whole lake to skate on. Nothing but glare ice all the way to the horizon. "If I don't tell Dad, then you've got to let him go."

"Gunnar's mine," Marianne said.

"He's lonely. He needs to be with other wolves."

"You said wolves aren't people. They don't have feelings like us."

"Maybe I was wrong," Johnny answered.

"It isn't fair," Marianne said. "I don't get to keep him and I don't get my jacket, either. I've given you half my money for the berries."

Johnny started to say something, then stopped. It wasn't fair. He knew it wasn't fair. "Maybe you could help Mom when she knits stuff and takes it into town to sell, or maybe when she makes..." He stopped.

"Go ahead, shoot him. See if I care," Marianne shouted. Then she turned around and ran back toward the cabin.

Johnny didn't know what to do. He sat down on the edge of the crevice with his legs dangling over. The wolf pup sat below him, looking up. Every so often the pup would cock his head to one side as if to ask, "What are you doing?" Sometimes he'd give a small yip to get Johnny's attention.

Johnny realized it wouldn't be so easy to shoot him. He didn't want the skates that badly.

"I shouldn't have come and sat here and talked to you all those times," he said. "I shouldn't have brought you all those mice."

The pup jumped up and put his front feet on the wall of the crevice.

When he got home, Johnny went into Marianne's room. He had his money jar with him.

"It isn't fair," he admitted. He counted out half the money from the berries and gave it to her. "You paid to keep him. I have to pay to let him go. I've been thinking. If we put down a ladder, he could climb up."

Marianne nodded. "Okay," she said.

"I've got a plan," Johnny said.

Together, they chopped down two spindly tamarack trees and lopped off the branches. Then Johnny notched them. Marianne nailed the branches into the notches. Together, they carried the ladder through the bush.

The wolf was sleeping when they got there. They

put the ladder down into the crevice.

"When we come back tomorrow, he'll be gone," Johnny said.

But when they came back the next day, the wolf was sitting at the bottom of the crevice, staring up at them.

"Stupid wolf," Johnny said. "Ladder. Ladder." He pointed at the ladder and made climbing motions.

"How is he supposed to know it's a ladder?" Marianne asked. She snapped her fingers. "I've got an idea."

They went back to the gut pile. They collected a bag of fish heads and tails. At the cabin they got a ball of string. They took everything back to the crevice. When they got there, Marianne didn't throw them down to the wolf.

"Aren't you going to feed him?" Johnny asked.

"Pull up the ladder," Marianne said. When the ladder was up, she tied a fish head to each rung. "Now put it down." She put the rest of the fish heads on the ground beside the top of the ladder.

When they came back the next day, the fish heads were all eaten and the wolf was gone.

"We don't have a wolf any more," Marianne said.

"He wasn't ours anyway," Johnny said. "We just had him for a little while."

"What about your skates?"

"I'll ask Dad if you and I can set one net close to shore this winter and sell the fish from it. You and I can split it."

"I wish he would come back," Marianne said. "I wish he could have been our friend."

"He's a wild animal," Johnny replied. "He's got to go away and be a wolf."

After that, when they saw tracks in the snow or in the sand, they always checked to see if it was their wolf who had made them. They knew when it was him because his injured leg turned slightly inward.

Sometimes when they were cleaning nets or playing catch, they'd feel like they were being watched. They would look at each other and then into the forest. Sometimes they thought they saw a shadow move or the glint of bright eyes. At night, especially in the winter when the moon was full and the snow was gold and purple and they heard a wolf call, they'd always stop to listen.

"Do you think he remembers us?" Marianne asked.

"Maybe," Johnny said. "Maybe not. But we'll always remember him."

BABYSITTING KWON LIN

"I hate this place," Richard said. His mother was doing up her hair. She was getting ready to go to work at Little Bo's. Little Bo's was a fast-food restaurant. It mostly served sandwiches and hot dogs and fries.

"Don't start that again," Richard's mother said. "We're not going back to Port Alberni."

Richard kicked the leg of the chair.

"Don't damage Mr. Yen's furniture," his mother said. She wet the tip of her finger with her tongue and smoothed down her eyebrows.

"Mr. Yen doesn't like me," Richard said.

"Mr. Yen is a good guy. He keeps the building clean and he lets us charge our groceries if we're short." His mother picked up her bag and slung it over her shoulder. "No coming into Bo's. He doesn't like the waitresses' kids hanging around." She blew him a kiss. "I'm nearly late," she said. The screen door banged behind her.

"I hate it here," Richard shouted. He picked up a pillow and was going to throw it across the room when he saw a movement on the balcony. It wasn't really a balcony. It was a landing for the fire escape. His mother insisted on calling it a balcony. On sunny days she took her foamy out there and tanned.

He ran to the window. There was no one there. He looked up just in time to see a leg disappear. He climbed out the window.

"Hey," he shouted. "This here's private property." He couldn't see who he was yelling at because the person had climbed onto the roof.

He thought maybe he should call Mr. Yen. There were plenty of thieves in Chinatown. If something wasn't nailed down, it disappeared. Sometimes even if it was nailed down, it disappeared.

Richard looked down into the alley. There was no one there. If it was a B&E there'd be a lookout. He started up the ladder to the roof. The metal steps burned his bare feet.

Mr. Yen had turned the roof into a garden. There were long tables filled with soil. In these were planted vegetables and flowers. Mr. Yen didn't allow anyone up here except Richard and his mom. After work he'd come up by himself and water and weed. Besides the tables there were large ceramic pots and a life-sized metal sculpture of a crane.

Richard scanned the rooftop. There was only one way off the roof and he was on it. He pulled himself over the ceramic tile wall, then slipped to his hands and knees so he could see under the tables. He crept along looking for feet. He circled the outside of the roof. No one. He crept along between the tables.

At last, he stood up. Maybe, he thought, he'd just imagined seeing someone.

He heard a movement behind him.

He spun around. A girl in black silk pajamas was standing in one of the large pots.

He was angry at having been tricked. "No one is supposed to come up here."

She raised herself out of the pot and slid to the roof.

"You're trespassing. You get out of here or I'll call the cops."

She plucked a carrot and took a bite out of it.

"Put that back," Richard ordered.

She bit off the rest of the carrot and flicked the carrot top at him.

"You!" Richard shouted. He started toward her and she ran around a corner. He chased her up and down and around the tables. They both stopped to catch their breath.

The girl was smaller than Richard but faster. The way she moved reminded him of the ferret he'd had at Port Alberni. It could change directions so quickly that there was no catching it.

The girl reached out and plucked a radish. Richard lunged at her. She slipped under a table, ran to the wall and climbed down. Richard raced down the ladder after her. When he got to the bottom, the alleyway was empty. The metal gate leading into the alley was closed. He turned and ran through the back door of the store, past the boxes of *bok choi* and sour melons.

"Mr. Yen," he shouted. "Someone was trespassing on your roof."

He ran around the counter. The girl in the black pajamas was sitting on a sack of rice.

"Ah," Mr. Yen said, "you have met my niece, Kwon Lin."

Mr. Yen spoke rapidly in Chinese. His niece stood up and bowed. Richard nodded back. She was full of tricks, he thought. She could appear and disappear. Like magic.

"She has come to live with me. She does not speak any English. Last week you said you wanted to earn money to buy your mother a present for her birthday. You can do so now." Richard thought Mr. Yen was going to say he could deliver groceries or sweep the store. Instead, Mr. Yen said, "Kwon Lin has not been well. She has come here to get better. You can take her with you. Show her the city. Teach her some English."

"Babysit?" Richard said.

"Yes," Mr. Yen replied. He gave one nod of his head, then went to see about a customer.

Richard tipped his head back and sighed loudly. He shook his head. He'd have to talk to his mother about this. He'd have to get her to explain to Mr. Yen that he couldn't be a sheep dog for some girl. His mom was good at straightening things out.

He turned and started out through the storage area at the back. When he looked around, Kwon Lin was right behind him. Richard stopped. She stopped. He took two steps. She took two steps.

"Whoa," Richard said. "Not today, okay? You stay here. I've got things to do."

He really didn't have anything to do. Since they'd moved to the apartment two months before, he'd barely gone outside. Instead, he watched TV and read comic books and tried to figure out how he could move back home. Every day he wrote a letter to his best friend, Gary, who still lived in Port Alberni. He saved up the letters and mailed them once a week.

Richard went outside and started up the ladder. Kwon Lin started up the ladder behind him. He climbed down. She climbed down and stood to one side.

"You wait here," he said. "I'll be right back." He pointed at her, then at the brick paving. He nodded. She stared at him.

He walked to the gate and smiled at her. He opened the gate, then darted around the corner and ran across the street. When he looked over his shoulder, Kwon Lin was right behind him. He stopped. She stopped in the middle of the road.

"Get out of the road," he yelled. "There are cars coming." He ran back, grabbed her arm and pulled her onto the sidewalk.

If only she could speak English, he thought. He could tell her to go away. He had to be careful, though. Mr. Yen was their landlord and he was giving them a break on the rent. If Richard did something to make Mr. Yen throw them out, his mother would kill him. With her bare hands.

"Okay," he said. "Fine."

He didn't know what to do. He didn't know any-

thing about Victoria. He didn't want to know anything about Victoria. He'd run away twice, each
time hitchhiking back to Port Alberni. His mother
had to come and drag him back.

"It's not our house any more," she said. "We had
to sell it. It's not your tree house any more. It's not
my living room any more. It's not our garage any
more. It's not our yard with our apple trees." Then
she'd started to cry.

Her being mad hadn't scared him. He knew she
loved him. But her crying scared him. It was like she
didn't know what to do and he didn't know what to
do. So he came back to the city with her and didn't
run away again.

"I hate Victoria," he said to Kwon Lin. She was
walking on his left and a step behind him. "I don't
know anything about it. I don't want to know anything about it."

What, he wondered, was he supposed to do with
her? He didn't know much about girls. It wasn't like
he had sisters or anything. The girls at his school
had been giggly and were always talking about
clothes and rock stars and things. Kwon Lin couldn't
even talk, and he doubted if she knew anything
about rock stars. Besides, she was younger than
him. At least, she looked younger.

He turned in at Market Square. Kwon Lin
stopped to study the quilts. Then they went into a

shop full of imported brass and carved sandalwood from India. They went into a shop full of books about sailing. In the square itself there was a band playing, so they stopped and listened. Richard put his hand in his pocket. He had a dollar twenty-five that he'd earned for carrying groceries the day before. He went and bought a drink. Kwon Lin followed him. He sipped at the drink.

"Have you got any money?" he asked. He held out the dime and two pennies he had left. Kwon Lin stared at him. He held out his drink. She ignored the straw.

He wished he'd made some friends. Then he'd have someone he could palm her off on. He could have introduced her to some girls. He at least would have had someone to complain to.

"If I was still at Port Alberni, I'd sic you on the nerds. You look smart. You'd fit right in."

"I'm not going to be a babysitter," he said to his mother that evening. "I won't do it. She's like a leech. She nearly followed me into the bathroom."

"Be nice to her," his mother said. They were eating hot dogs that had been left over at Bo's. There was leftover kraut and fries as well.

In their house in Port Alberni, they'd had cinnamon toast and grapefruit for breakfast. Bacon and eggs.

Richard didn't want his mom to cry again, so he shut up. But he lay awake thinking up ways of escaping from Kwon Lin. The problem was there were only two exits. One was through the alley. The other was through the grocery store. One end of the alley ended on the street. The other ended in a square space filled with piles of junk. It was surrounded by the brick back walls of buildings. There were doors but most of them were permanently locked.

"I don't belong here, see," he said to Kwon Lin the next morning. "I belong out there, in the country. I used to have a dog and cat. They belong to Gary now. There were raccoons in the yard every night. We used to feed them out of my bedroom window."

They were sitting on the stone steps at the harbor, watching a juggler toss burning sticks in the air. They'd just inspected all the boats. Richard hadn't wanted to look at the boats, but he was desperate. He couldn't just stay in the apartment all day with her there cross-legged watching him. It would drive him crazy.

When Richard said he was taking Kwon Lin to the boat show, Mr. Yen had given him ten dollars to get them something to eat and drink.

"Get something healthy, Richard," Mr. Yen had said. Mr. Yen's store was filled with healthy things.

He had a glass counter filled with pills made from antlers and gall bladders and hooves and weird plants. People were always coming in to tell him how sick they were and to ask him for something that would help.

After the juggler was finished, Richard and Kwon Lin went back onto Government Street. He thought it was time to get a sandwich or a piece of pizza. Kwon Lin stopped at the cart where three men were selling large ice-cream cones. One man took money, another filled large sugar cones with ice cream and strawberries and the third man handed customers the cones.

After a couple of minutes, Richard wiggled his finger at Kwon Lin to follow him. He held his hand up to his mouth and made biting motions. She looked at him, then looked back at the cart with the cones. Richard waited, then went over to her.

"Kwon Lin," he said and pointed down the street with his thumb. Kwon Lin didn't move. "Your uncle said something healthy. Besides, these cost too much. If we buy these, we won't have any money left for anything else."

She turned her head away from him and stared at the cart. It was like he had ceased to exist. He was so frustrated he wanted to stamp his feet.

"No," he said. "Don't you understand no?" She ignored him. "Oh, for the love of mud."

He bought a cone and gave it to her. She ate it as they walked down Government Street. She stopped again in front of a shop window. In the window were white bears wearing red Mountie jackets and red Mountie hats. She wouldn't leave for a long time.

That night, when they were sitting in the roof garden watching the tourists walk by, Richard said, "I can't do it, Mom," he said. "It's too hard."

"Would you like to try being a waitress at Bo's?"

"She can't even speak English. She's too dumb."

"Learn some Chinese, then."

"Me? Chinese? You can't be serious. I can't learn Chinese. Nobody talks Chinese in Port Alberni."

"How smart do you have to be to learn ten words?"

After his mother went out, Richard kicked the pillow so hard it flew out the window onto the landing. Why should he have to learn ten words?

"I want to learn ten words of Chinese," he said to Mr. Yen the next morning.

"No such language as Chinese," Mr. Yen said. "Many dialects. Most speak Cantonese or Mandarin. What ten words do you want to know?"

"I don't know."

Mr. Yen said something very quickly. It sounded like gobbledy-gook. "That's how you say I don't know."

"No, that's not what I meant," Richard replied. "I haven't thought of what ten words I need most for Kwon Lin."

"No might be a good start," Mr. Yen said. "Especially when it comes to ice-cream cones that cost three dollars and fifty cents. Then yes. You'll think of others."

Mr. Yen told him how to say yes and no. *Hila* and *mo*. Richard kept repeating them. When he said them to Kwon Lin, though, she looked at him like he was still speaking English.

"It's your accent," Sam Wong said. Sam ran a souvenir shop. It was crammed to the ceiling with boxes of shells and beads and dolls and joss sticks and little porcelain animals.

"I haven't got an accent," Richard said. "That's ridiculous."

Sam said *hila*. Richard repeated it after him. Sam repeated it. Richard repeated it. They repeated it until a customer came in.

"They say I've got an accent," Richard said to his mother.

They were eating noodle soup with fish balls. "Kwon Lin made it," his mother said. "She's younger than you."

"I'm not learning to make soup," he said. "Enough's enough."

Mr. Yen had given him two dollars for babysitting Kwon Lin. He used it to call Gary.

"What's happening to me?" he said. "They've got me talking Chinese and eating noodles."

He took Kwon Lin to Beacon Hill Park. Mr. Yen had given them a picnic lunch. Richard carried it in his knapsack.

They walked around the park, looking at the flowers. Richard had a loaf of stale bread his mother had brought from work. The sign said not to feed the ducks, but they fed them anyway. They stopped by the petting zoo to look at the donkey and the chickens. They sat with their feet in a fountain. They walked down to the cliffs. Two men were flying remote-control airplanes. The planes zoomed out over the ocean, then came swooping back in.

Richard and Kwon Lin took their lunch down a path to the beach and sat on the sand among the logs and ate all sorts of things Richard had never seen before.

"I'm not eating chicken feet," he said.

Kwon Lin held out a dumpling. "Yes, Richard," she said. She sounded like she was hissing when she said it. He wondered if that's what he sounded like when he said something in Cantonese.

As they watched the boats sail by, he said, "I hate it here. I don't belong here. It's a nice place, all right. I mean, look at this ocean and the beach and all this stuff. It'd be fine, I guess, if my dad was here but he's up in Yellowknife. I guess..." He had to stop because it hurt too much to say it. He swallowed, then looked away. "I guess he doesn't want to be my dad any more. He didn't even say goodbye. I came home from school and he was gone and that was it. There was just my mom and me and we couldn't keep the house. I didn't know what to do. I wanted to get a job but they wouldn't let me because I have to go to school. He could have at least said good-bye."

He didn't feel much like eating after that, so he just sat there and threw stones into the water. Not angry throwing like he'd done after his dad had left. More like hopeless throwing, watching the stones disappear. They were there and then they were gone, just like his father.

The next day while he was helping sweep out the store, Mr. Yen said, "Tell me your ten words."

"*Hila*. Hello. *Mo*. No. *Nay ho ma?* How are you? *Kay ni shi*. Stand here. *Kay goy do*. Stand there. *Choy ni shi*. Sit here. *Choy goy do*. Sit there. *M-ho moi*. Don't touch. *Lay la*. You come."

"That is more than ten words," Mr. Yen said.

"I've learned fourteen words," Richard said, "but Kwon Lin has only learned two."

Mr. Yen was stamping prices on little golden boxes of tea. He stopped. "She has learned two?"

"She knows how to say, 'Yes, Richard.' But that's all."

Mr. Yen grabbed his arm. He bent down. "She has said, 'Yes, Richard'?"

"I asked her if she wanted to jump in the ocean. She said, 'Yes, Richard.' I asked her if she wanted to eat worms. She said, 'Yes, Richard.'"

Mr. Yen let go of his arm. He patted Richard on the shoulder, then gave him a box of candy wrapped in rice paper.

Richard went into Sam's souvenir shop. "I've learned a whole bunch of words of Cantonese. No one thinks that's amazing, but Kwon Lin learns to say two words and Mr. Yen looks like he's going to have a heart attack."

Sam patted his mouth and nodded. "She has said something?"

Richard snorted. "I don't get it."

Sam handed him a small clay dragon. "You take this for luck, Richard."

"Crazy," Richard said to his mother. "They're all crazy. Anybody can learn to say yes. *Oui. Da. Si.* It's not so hard."

"It's not that," his mother explained. She stopped filing her nails. "Her parents were killed in an earthquake. So was her sister. She was trapped inside a building that had fallen down. For five days. She hasn't said anything since they found her. Her mother was Mr. Yen's sister."

"Nobody told me," Richard said. "Somebody should have told me."

"I didn't know," his mother replied. "Not until I went into the store today. I'm not keeping any secrets."

♣

"Go fly kite," Mr. Yen said when Richard went to buy milk the next morning.

"You don't want me around?" he asked.

Mr. Yen reached behind the counter. He took out a package. "Chinese kite. Look good at Clover Point. Nobody got kite like this."

Richard took the kite upstairs, but the apartment was too small. He needed a bigger space. He went back down and asked Mr. Yen if he could go onto the roof.

"You take Kwon Lin," Mr. Yen said. She appeared from behind a shelf filled with blue bowls. She had pink barrettes in her hair. They made her look even more like a little kid.

Richard looked at Mr. Yen, then at Kwon Lin. "She'll just get in the way," he said. "Oh, all right. Sure. She can come."

There was a flat piece of roof that didn't have any plants. They spread the parts of the kite there. Kwon Lin had brought a bottle of glue and a roll of string. There was a picture of the kite on the package but the instructions were in Chinese.

Richard's mother came up to look but she knew nothing about kites. If it had been a triple decker with fries she could have built it right away.

Mr. Yen came up. He watched what they were doing, then nodded and disappeared. Richard assumed they were on the right track.

"If my dad was here, he'd know how to put this together," Richard ranted in exasperation. "My dad can make anything. He made me a swing out of a tire. He cut the tire to look like a horse. That's when I was little. He made a picnic table and chairs. He built our cupboards. That's what he was doing in Calgary. Now he's out of work. There's a recession. That means there's no jobs. If there was a job, he'd send us some money."

He couldn't make any sense out of all the bits and pieces. He tried fitting them one way, then another. The picture wasn't much help. Kwon Lin picked up the package and read the instructions. She waved him away, then started sorting everything out. She worked neatly and quickly, making piles of wood and paper. When she had finished, the circles of material stretched across the roof.

Together, they began to fit the pieces together and glue on the paper.

"I'm sorry about your folks," Richard said. "I'm sorry they got killed and everything. I wish you could talk English. I wish I could speak Chinese."

It took them all day to build the kite. When they were finished, it was too late to go to Clover Point. Richard went down to get Mr. Yen. He came onto the roof and nodded. He looked at the sky. It was bright red over the Sooke Hills.

"Tomorrow will be good day," he said. "We go to Clover Point."

"We?" Richard thought. He'd wondered how they were going to get the kite to Clover Point. It was too big for the bus. If there was a breeze, carrying it would be difficult even with two of them. He wondered if Mr. Yen was going to walk with them.

The next morning Mr. Yen knocked on the door. He didn't have on his white apron. Instead, he was dressed in a gray suit and tie and a hat. Richard had only seen a hat like that in the movies.

"We go," Mr. Yen said.

In the alleyway, there was a large yellow car. An antique, Richard thought. With fenders and running boards. He was glad he didn't know anyone in Victoria. He didn't want anyone to see him.

They carefully fitted the kite into the back seat. Then they sat in the front with Kwon Lin between them.

When they got to Clover Point, there were waves on the ocean. The tops of the trees were moving. Mr. Yen parked. Then they carried the kite to the grassy area. They laid the kite out. With all the pieces attached, the dragon was enormous. Mr. Yen tied two lines to it. Each of the lines had a handle.

"Me show," Mr. Yen said. "No want dragon to carry boy to China."

"I can fly a kite," Richard said. "My dad showed me how."

Mr. Yen went to the front of the kite and pulled it so the front tipped up. The dragon rippled, then settled. Mr. Yen tipped up the head again and pulled. This time when the dragon rippled, it also rose into the air. Mr. Yen held fast to the lines, pulling first on one, then the other.

The dragon began to walk across the sky. The dragon shook its head, it circled, it dove toward them, then climbed. Finally, Mr. Yen brought it back to earth.

"I go now," he said, handing Richard the handles. "I come back at twelve to pick you up. Just remember, Chinese dragon is very strong. It can take you far away."

Richard pulled on the handles. Nothing happened. He tried to remember what Mr. Yen had done. He stopped and shut his eyes, trying to see again. Richard lifted his hands like Mr. Yen, and the kite tipped up slightly. He tried again but could not catch the wind.

Kwon Lin went to the kite and lifted up the head. She raised it over her shoulders. Richard could feel it pull against the wind. Kwon Lin let go and ducked away. The kite rose into the sky. Richard was glad of the handles. The dragon was strong. He felt it could lift him from the ground. It might not carry him to China, but it might drag him into the ocean. He pulled harder on the right handle and the dragon bobbed and weaved, then slowly turned. He hauled on the left handle.

He flew the kite for half an hour, learning to make it weave like a snake.

Suddenly, the wind gusted. Richard felt his feet lift from the ground.

"Kwon Lin," he cried. "Help!"

She ran and grabbed one of the handles. Between them they held the kite as it bobbed and wove.

"Hold on, hold on," he said. They were being dragged toward the water. He pulled with all his might on the left handle. The dragon made a long curve, then dove toward the earth.

When the wind died down, they flew the kite again, drawing it in long, dipping circles. Both of them watched the water for the sign of more gusts of wind, but there were none.

When Mr. Yen came to get them, he said, "You like flying kite, eh? Not too much wind?"

"No," Richard said. "It's just fine. A light breeze, that's all."

Mr. Yen said something to Kwon Lin and

Richard could tell he was asking her about the kite flying. She looked at Richard and even though he didn't understand the words, the expression on her face said she was saying the same thing he had said.

"You and me," Richard said the next day when he was showing her Thunderbird Park, "we're sort of the same, you know." He'd got so he talked to her even though she didn't say anything back. He thought maybe that way she'd learn. When they were sightseeing, he pointed at things and said their names. That's how Sam was teaching him some more words of Cantonese. If it worked for him, it should work for her.

"See, we're both living here and this is no place for us. My mom says you lived in the country, too. We're not city kids, you and me. We don't belong here. As soon as I can, I'm moving back to Port Alberni. Maybe I can't live in my old house, but I can get another place. You can't just move people from one place to the other. They caught a cougar around here, you know, a mountain lion. Right on the parking lot. They took it back to the bush. It couldn't live here. I mean, there's lots of poodles and cats and rats and things for it to eat, but it still couldn't live here. It had to go back."

That afternoon when they walked downtown, Kwon Lin stopped in front of the shop window with the white bears in Mountie uniforms. There were only three left. Richard sighed and sat on one of the concrete planters and waited until she was ready to leave.

The next day, as they were sitting on the roof, Richard noticed a bird high above.

"Look," he said excitedly and pointed up. "A falcon."

As they watched, it dove straight down until it hit a pigeon. The pigeon fell. The falcon swooped and caught its tumbling body.

"Look, look, it stooped. Now it's going to its nest." He thought it would fly toward Metchosin, toward the Sooke Hills. Instead, it made a circle above them and dropped down to the top ledge of the building opposite them.

"A nest." Richard grasped Kwon Lin's shoulder. "See? His mate's on the nest. They must have eggs."

"You're sure it's a falcon?" his mother asked him later.

"Yes, absolutely," he replied. "It's blue-backed and has a mustache. You mustn't tell anyone. Promise?"

His mother crossed her first two fingers. That was her way of saying she promised.

Mr. Yen came to look the next day. He brought his binoculars. The four of them sat behind the low wall at the front of the roof. After that they watched the falcons every day.

One afternoon when they looked, they saw two tiny heads bobbing up and down.

It was just after that Mr. Yen said, "Kwon Lin go now."

"Go where?" Richard asked. He thought Mr. Yen was going to take Kwon Lin to some event.

"Home," Mr. Yen said. "China."

"She can't go to China," Richard said. "She lives here now."

"Just for a little time," Mr. Yen said. "Maybe she come and visit again. Now she goes to Uncle and Auntie. No good here. Mr. Yen an old bachelor uncle. She need Mommy and Daddy. Just okay here for emergency."

"But this is her home now."

"You've been good friend to her. She needed friend. Maybe you like to come to airport. Say good-bye."

The next day Richard put on his good jeans and shirt and waited at the bottom of the stairs. Mr. Yen backed his big yellow car out of the garage. Kwon Lin's suitcase was in the back seat. She sat between them.

Richard didn't care if people stared at the old-fashioned car. He was silently practicing saying good-bye in Cantonese.

At the airport, a stewardess came to lead Kwon Lin away. Richard took a Mountie teddy bear out of his pack and gave it to her. She gave him a hug, then she left through Security.

On the way back, neither he nor Mr. Yen said anything. Richard went up to the roof. When his mom came home, she came up and joined him. She'd brought barbecued ribs and fries from work.

"How're the birds doing?" she asked. "It must be tough raising a family on the ledge of a building instead of on a cliff."

"Yeah," Richard agreed. "But they're doing okay. The chicks are eating. They're adapting. The ledge isn't very big, but they're making do with what they've got."

NOT LONELY

Tom was eating his favorite lunch, spaghetti, when his mother said, "There's no fish in the south end of the lake this year."

"Oh, yeah," he replied. He wasn't really paying attention. He was wondering if there was anyone at the playground that he could play baseball with.

"We're going to have to fish up north."

"North," he said, looking up. There was no school at the fish camp up north. He'd never even been there, though he'd heard lots of talk about it. There were cabins and a cook shack and ice house and sheds for cleaning and packing fish. There were moose and bears.

"I'll have to cook," Tom's mother said. "Your dad's got a lot of men working for him this year."

Tom swallowed his spaghetti. "When are we leaving?"

"You've got to go to school."

"Me?" He looked around the kitchen. "I can't stay by myself." He was thinking about what he could cook. Toast, boiled eggs, canned spaghetti. He made good peanut butter and banana sandwiches.

"You're staying with the Thompsons."

"But I can help," Tom protested. "I've helped Dad pack fish. I can help in the kitchen. I can peel potatoes. I can do lots of things."

"The Thompsons have a big-screen TV. You like their dog, Snorri."

"You don't want me to go with you," Tom said.

"We don't want to leave you behind. But there are no other kids at the camp." His mother handed him a calendar with pictures of horses on it. "Here's the day we're coming back," she said. She crossed her heart. "I promise." She'd marked the day by drawing a heart with a smiley face inside it.

Tom bicycled down to the dock to watch his parents leave. It took his father all morning to load the boat with food and nets and anchors and drums of gasoline.

When everything was ready, his mother gave him a hug. His father shook his hand and ruffled his hair. Then they got on board. The freight boat was towing a string of smaller boats. As the boat pulled away from the dock, Tom's mother waved, but he didn't wave back. He stood and watched until the boats became little specks on the horizon and then disappeared altogether. Then he got on his bicycle and rode to the Thompsons.

If his parents didn't need him, he said to himself, then he didn't need them. He'd rather stay with the Thompsons anyway. Mrs. Thompson let him play games on her computer, and Mr. Thompson had promised to take him to the city to watch a football game.

The first week Tom watched cartoons on the big TV every afternoon after school. The second week he took Snorrie for long walks. Snorrie was a black Lab and he loved the water. Tom threw sticks into the lake so Snorrie could swim out and bring them back.

Staying with the Thompsons was okay but on his way from school, Tom sometimes forgot and turned in at the gate to his house. Then he'd remember and stop and stare at the house. It usually looked happy. Now it looked forlorn. Neglected. It needed his mother to sweep and dust and tidy and love it.

Sometimes he'd sit on the steps and pretend that he was waiting for his mother to return from shopping. Sometimes he'd walk around the yard picking up papers and plastic that had got caught in the caragana hedge or in the garden.

One day Mrs. Thompson saw him tidying up the yard.

"Are you lonely?" she asked him.

"No," he said. "Dad likes things tidy."

He noticed that his mother's hollyhocks had all turned brown. Every summer she watched for the big pink and white flowers to open. When she was home she always collected the seeds in a plastic bag so she could plant hollyhocks the next year.

Tom got a plastic bag from Mrs. Thompson and collected the seeds from the brown, dry pods. He tucked the seeds away in his suitcase.

At the end of the fourth week, Mrs. Thompson noticed his calendar. He had marked off each day with a big black X.

"Are you sure you're not lonely?" Mrs. Thompson asked him.

"No," he said. "There's lots to do."

On his way from school, he noticed that the

birches were shedding their leaves. He borrowed the Thompsons' rake. He raked the leaves into a pile, then put them into the compost box.

One Saturday when the weather was so bad that Tom couldn't go out, Mr. Thompson saw him standing at the window. He was watching the wind and the rain whip the spruce trees back and forth. Some branches had broken off.

"The weather is terrible," Mr. Thompson said. "I've never seen such bad wind and such high waves. The waves were breaking right over the dock today."

"So what," Tom said. "I'm not on the lake. It's not my problem."

The next day he noticed that nearly everything in his mom's garden had turned brown. He borrowed Mr. Thompson's pitchfork and dug up the potatoes and put them in a box. He pulled up the bean vines. He put the potatoes in the back shed, the vines in the compost.

"Are you sure you're not lonely?" Mr. Thompson asked as they played catch with a football on the sixth weekend.

"No," Tom said. "Being on my own will help me grow up faster. Everybody says so."

The next Sunday he pried open a basement window. He got his comic books out of his closet and lay on his bed and read them even though it was freezing in the house. He made himself cocoa with sugar and water. It wasn't as good as when his mom made it. When she made cocoa, it was hot and had milk in it. He wrapped himself in a comforter and read every one of his comic books.

"Your parents will be back next week," Mrs. Thompson said.

"I've hardly noticed the time go by," Tom replied. He went back to the house that weekend and got out the vacuum cleaner and vacuumed the floor. He found some blue asters in the garden. He put them in a glass with water and set them on the kitchen table. He swept the back porch and the front porch.

He had been saving his allowance money. He went to the corner store and bought a carton of milk and a loaf of bread. He bought some butter. He had some money left over so he bought some chocolates. He put those beside the flowers.

When he got back to the Thompsons, he checked the calendar. All the days had been crossed off. Today was the day with the heart drawn on it. His mother had crossed her heart and promised that they'd be back on this day.

Tom took out his suitcase and packed his clothes. He carried his suitcase downstairs and put it beside the front door.

"I could carry it to our place," he said.

"I think you'd better wait until they show up. They said they were going to come straight here," Mr. Thompson said.

"I could turn the heat up at the house."

"Maybe they won't be able to make it right on time. The weather's been pretty terrible. The radio said there are some high winds on the north end of the lake."

"They promised," Tom said. He already had on his jacket.

"You're going to get awfully warm with that jacket on," Mrs. Thompson said. "Why not take it off while we have tea? I've made some scones and we've got strawberry jam."

Tom sat beside the front window all day. Sometimes he went outside so he could see farther down the road. Mrs. Thompson made fish and chips for supper. Then it got dark. Tom kept watching, certain that each set of headlights on the road would be them.

"Time to go to bed," Mrs. Thompson said. "School tomorrow."

"They should be here pretty soon."

"I don't think they'd travel at night in this weather," Mr. Thompson replied. "Your dad's pretty careful. He's not going to take unnecessary risks."

Tom carried his suitcase back upstairs. He took

out his pajamas but he didn't put them on. He lay on top of the bed, listening for the sound of a truck door shutting.

In the morning, when Mrs. Thompson woke him up, he was lying on the bed still dressed. Outside the wind howled and sleet rattled against the window.

The next day the sleet and snow had stopped but there was a lot of wind. When Tom went to the lake, large dark-gray waves were breaking over the dock, sending up huge walls of white spray. He made a shelter out of some fish boxes and sat inside it, watching the horizon. He remembered all the stories he'd heard his father tell about traveling through storms. He watched until it was supper time, then rode his bicycle back to the Thompsons.

The next afternoon Mrs. Thompson met him at the school. "There's a boat coming," she said. They went down to the dock together.

The waves were still large but the wind had died down. Instead of crashing against the dock, the waves rolled along it, making a sighing sound. During the night the temperature had fallen. The dock was thick with ice. The water looked black.

They watched as a boat rose and fell on the waves. Sometimes it seemed to be completely out of the water. Then it would dive down into a trough and disappear completely. It was hard to tell whether it was his dad's boat. The boats all looked the same. Gray and white with square cabins.

Every seventh wave was larger, rising up so high sometimes that their crests rode above the dock. When they broke against the shore, it was with a long, deep roar.

As they watched, the boat slowly worked its way south, past the entrance to the harbor, then came around so that it could go directly into the entrance between the south and north docks. It seemed as if the boat was hardly moving, but gradually it grew larger. Even when it was safely through the entrance into the quiet water of the harbor, it was impossible to tell whose boat it was. The boat was covered in ice.

The crew members threw out ropes and tied up to the dock. They were dressed in black oilers: rubber pants and jackets and hats. The hats had large brims and were tied under their chins. It was impossible to tell who was on the boat.

Tom wanted to run to see, but Mrs. Thompson said it was too dangerous. Water was running over the dock and ice coated everything. A large wave could sweep him into the harbor, or he might slip on the ice and tumble down one of the chutes into the water.

Finally, the crew managed to reach the foot of

the dock. It wasn't Tom's mother and father.

"Have you seen Helgi and Jean?" Mrs. Thompson asked.

"No one on the lake but us, missus," one of the crew members said. "We shouldn't 'a' been but one of the fellas isn't well. We've been chopping ice off all day. We thought she was going to turn turtle."

His oilers were covered with ice and there was ice hanging from his mustache. He'd added that he'd heard that a boat had sunk but he hadn't heard whose it was or what had happened to the crew.

"They'll be fine," Mrs. Thompson said. "Your dad's not reckless. He'll stay anchored until the weather improves."

That night Mrs. Thompson gave Tom an extra slice of chocolate cake at supper, then got him to unpack his suitcase.

The next day Tom couldn't concentrate at school. He kept looking out the window. He thought if his parents got back safely, they'd come to the school to get him.

He went to the house to check on the flowers and the milk and the bread and the chocolates. He tried the lights to see if they still worked.

After he was in bed that night, he wondered what would happen to him if his parents didn't come back. If his parents weren't paying for his room and board, he didn't think the Thompsons would let him stay, and he didn't have any money of his own. He wondered if he'd have to live with a foster family. One of the kids in his class lived with a foster family.

At two A.M. he woke up. He didn't know why he woke up. He listened for the steady roar of the waves. He couldn't hear it.

When he listened more carefully, he heard voices. He sat up. He slipped out of bed. He opened the door and crept down the hallway.

There were his parents sitting at the kitchen table. They were dressed in blue jeans and heavy sweaters. Their parkas were hanging on the backs of their chairs. They were drinking tea.

Tom didn't move but his mother turned around and saw him. She smiled and opened her arms. He went running to her and gave her a hug. Then his father gave him a hug.

"I'm sorry we were so long getting back," his father said. "But the weather was terrible and we had to wait until it was safe."

"I'll bet you've been really lonely," his mother said.

"Yes," Tom said, "but not any more."

"Xplthgrdkja," Billy said. He tugged at Sam's shirt.

"What?" Sam asked.

"Xplthgrdkja," Billy repeated.

"What's that?" Sam asked. He was busy searching the Web for someone interesting to chat with.

"Xplthgrdkja," Billy said in a frustrated voice. "Xplthgrdkja!"

"I don't know what you want," his cousin said, brushing his hand away. "You've got to speak more clearly."

His name was William Harry, but his parents always called him Billy. They only called him William Harry when he was trying to catch the goldfish or when he was pulling on the cat's tail.

"Xplthgrdkja," he shouted. He waved his arms. "Xplthgrdkja!"

"There's no need to shout," Sam said. "Shouting's not polite. That's an outside voice. Go ask Carol. She talks weird."

Carol was watching a football game, a baseball game and a hockey game on three different TVs. Her major goal in life was to become a jock. That's why she had both feet on the coffee table and was drinking a soft drink out of a can. She never wore anything but sweatpants and tops. If anyone turned on the program "Fashion File," she screamed and ran out of the room.

"Wait a minute," she said. "They're just going to a commercial."

The remotes were lined up in a wire holder set on the coffee table. Carol punched three mute buttons.

"Okay," she said to Billy. "What's the problem? You've got ninety seconds to make your point."

"Xplthgrdkja!"

"Look in the fridge," Carol said. She believed that whatever anyone wanted could be found in the fridge. When she wasn't jogging, playing soccer, hockey, baseball, rowing sculls, weight-lifting or swimming, she was eating. If it couldn't be found in the fridge, it could be found in the mall. She was the Mall Queen. She'd have thought she'd died and gone to heaven if she could have got a job in a sporting goods shop in Mayfair Mall.

She went into the kitchen and opened the fridge door. She held up milk, bread, lettuce, tofu, beets, radishes, cabbage, catsup, mustard, pickles, wieners, carrots and horseradish. Billy shook his head.

They went back into the living-room. Every game was in the midst of a play.

"I tried," she shouted to Sam. "He's your cousin, too. You find out what he wants."

Sam dragged Billy onto his lap. "Let's see if we can find it on the Web," he said. He believed that everything anyone could ever want was on the Web. It was just a matter of finding the right links. He typed in kid games, kid psychology, kid food, kid toys, kid music. Home pages flashed by.

Billy started to cry.

"Okay, okay," Sam said. If there was one thing he couldn't stand, it was tears. When he was little, he was afraid that if someone really cried, all their insides would run out and they'd wrinkle. If he saw really old people on the bus, he'd say to his mother, "Cried and cried." He got the idea from watching her dry tomatoes and apples. You took out all the liquid and they wrinkled.

Sam quit looking at the screen. He would never be able to explain a wrinkled four-year-old.

"He's crying," Sam yelled, but he knew it was no use. Carol shaved her head and had her nose pierced without any anesthetic. She said she was going to start taking karate so she could break bricks with her bare hands. Little kids wrinkling wouldn't faze her.

"Look, kid," Sam said. "There's nothing out there that isn't in here." He tapped the computer. "You've just got to tell me what you want. Then, *vavroom!* Down the Information Highway. I mean, we can find it even if it's in Australia or Mozambique."

"Xplthgrdkja!" Billy said and stamped his foot.

Reluctantly, Sam hit Close, Close, Close, Start.

"Stupid," he said, "to hit Start to stop. Badly designed port for cyberspace."

Outside, they hesitated on the front steps. Sam blinked and put on his shades.

"Bright," he said. "Bad UVs. You sure you want to do this?" He reached out and snapped his mouse finger but nothing happened. "I guess we've got to walk," he said.

They checked the library. "Archaic, Billy, archaic. Full of dust mites." Sam sneezed. He looked at the rows of books. All the people lined up borrowing books. "Slow processor, big memory." They went to the desk marked Information.

"He wants something," Sam said. "I've tried narrowing the search but..." He shrugged. "Come on, Billy, tell her."

"Xplthgrdkja!" Billy said.

The librarian had him repeat it a number of times. They even toured the children's book section.

"Wrong search engine," Sam said when they were back on the sidewalk.

They saw their family doctor coming out of his office. He checked Billy's pulse and felt his forehead and looked at his tongue and declared that the word didn't indicate that there was anything physically wrong with him.

They dropped by the college. Sam's father was a professor. He knew a lot of odd bits of information. Unfortunately, he was busy teaching.

The professor with the office next door asked them in. She had a prodigious pile of books.

"Xplthgrdkja!" Billy said.

The professor listened to the word. She had books on her walls and books in piles nearly to the ceiling.

"It could be an ancient language," she said. "Hebrew or Greek or Latin. Let me check." She pulled down so many books that there was a great cloud of dust, but none of them contained Xplthgrdkja.

"It probably isn't a word at all," the professor said. "Perhaps he has a speech impediment or was traumatized when he was born."

Billy stamped both feet in exasperation. "Xplthgrdkja," he said quite loudly.

After that they went to the corner store to get an orange popsicle. Billy said Xplthgrdkja to people buying milk and bread and magazines. One of the grocery clerks said he thought he'd had some of that a week ago but they were out of it now. He thought it might be an imported fruit. A lady pinching peaches suggested it might be some sort of South American vegetable too exotic for a corner grocery. She suggested they go downtown to the multicultural fair. There, she said, people could translate any language in the world.

"How can you want anything?" Sam said. "You've got more toys than Toys R Us. You've even got Batman sheets."

Billy's eyes filled up with tears.

"Okay, okay," Sam said. "Don't wrinkle." He had this fear that when his aunt returned, she'd find this little wrinkled kid. "We'll go downtown." He wondered what he was saying. He hadn't been downtown in months. Of course, he'd been downtown on the Web. There were street maps and home pages for businesses. You could tour the city.

As he paid their bus fare, he was appalled by how difficult it all was. "Not even 1200 baud," he said to Billy. "Like power outage. Like system shutdown." The bus lurched and bumped along the road.

They got off at Centennial Square.

The place was crowded. People in brightly colored costumes were dancing on a stage. A crowd was sitting on the concrete steps. Sam and Billy wove their way through the crowd. In front of the ethnic food booths, it was nearly impossible to move.

"Don't get lost," Sam said, and he took Billy's hand. Billy was staring at girl eating a large piece of something brown. She was wearing a gypsy costume and big gold earrings.

"What's that?" Sam asked.

"Elephant ears," she said.

"Gross," Sam replied. He had visions of herds of elephants with no ears running around Africa.

"Try it," the girl said. She tore off a piece. "It's fried bread with sugar and cinnamon."

Sam tore his piece in half. He gave a piece to Billy.

"Come on," she said. "Hurry. The music is starting." She crooked her finger at them. They followed. She stopped in front of the stage.

"Take my hand," she said.

Sam looked wildly around, then grasped her hand. He was holding onto Billy with his other hand.

"Watch my feet. Do what I do."

"What?" Sam said. "I can't dance. I do computers. I've never danced in my life." There was a line of adult dancers on the stage behind them, dancing to the music. The girl lifted one foot, swung it, then put it back where it had been before. Sam imitated her. Billy was swinging his foot, too.

"You'll do fine," the girl said. "My name's Amanda. This dance is a lesnoto." It was nearly all kids sitting in front of the stage. "Join in," she called to them. "Go to the back of the line." Kids started jumping up and forming a line.

"Cancel program," Sam said.

"I'm from Hungary," Amanda told him. "Where are you from?"

"Here," Sam said desperately.

"If you can use a computer, you can dance. Just think of it as simple foot programming."

By the time the dance finished, Sam had figured out the step. Billy just happily swung his feet in rhythm to the music.

"Now," Amanda said, "for being such a good sport, I'll buy you an elephant ear."

"Ugh!" Sam said, thinking of all those elephants with hearing aids. Billy was tugging on his hand, trying to follow Amanda. "Carol would kill me if she knew I let you eat fried bread," Sam told him. Carol ate Power Bars, raw broccoli, trail mix, red meat.

While they were eating their elephant ears, Amanda introduced them to some of the other dancers. He'd had Billy say Xplthgrdkja and she asked everyone if they knew what it meant. They talked to dancers from Thailand and Denmark and Croatia and China.

"I think it's a foreign word," Sam explained. "Something he's picked up from TV or daycare."

None of the dancers knew what the word was, but they asked people who asked other people. Sam ended up talking to a woman who had escaped from Vietnam in an open boat, a man who had a Ph.D. in physics but who was working as a janitor, a Russian ballerina, a German artist.

As they inched their way through the crowd, a clown blew up a long and skinny balloon and tied it in a circle so Billy could wear it on his head. A juggler juggled bright-red balls while he rode around on a unicycle. A musician played "Jingle Bells" on a bunch of glasses filled with water.

Billy tugged on Sam's hand. They checked out the booths crammed with things they'd never seen before.

Billy picked up a cloth tiger covered in sequins.

"Not enough bucks," Sam said. He showed Billy the inside of his wallet. "We'll have to get the parents down here with plastic." He held up a wooden mask with fierce white eyes and blue lips. "Even Carol might like it here." Instead of dancers, there were now people in black pajamas demonstrating kick-boxing. They had shaved heads. "She'll feel right at home."

Just before they left, they sat on a bench to eat an ice cream. An old man with a long white beard and pink turban sat down beside them. He leaned forward on his cane.

"Xplthgrdkja," Billy said and leaned back against the bench.

"What does he say?" the man in the pink turban asked.

"I don't know," Sam said. "That's why we came today. To find out what he wants. But no one's been able to figure it out."

"I know that word," the old man said.

"You do?"

"Yes, surely," the old man said. "I remember hearing children say it. I don't think adults can say it. They've forgotten how. Sometimes even young people forget."

"So it's East Indian. He must have been watching that TV channel," Sam said.

"No, I don't think so," the old man said. "I've lived all over the world and I've heard children say it in every country."

When they got home, Sam's father was watching TV and his mom was writing a report. Billy was so tired that Sam had to carry him piggyback all the way from the bus stop.

"Did you find out what he wanted?" their father said. Carol had told him that the Brothers Grimm had gone on a quest.

"Sam," she'd said, "will be lucky if he finds his way back. If the cops pick them up and ask where he lives, he'll give them his URL."

"You went downtown," Sam's mother said. She had three reports, two speeches and forty-seven letters to write.

"Poor links," Sam replied. "Music. Not as pro as off my sound system and the dancing's not, like, the Bolshoi on CD." He was listening to the lesnoto in his head again, replaying it, hearing the dancers yelling and stamping. He licked his lips. He could still taste the cinnamon and sugar. Before they left, the man in the turban had told him a story about catching cobras with his bare hands.

"How do you do it?" Sam had asked.

"Carefully. Very carefully," the man had replied, making him laugh.

Billy went upstairs for a nap. Sam sat on the bed

beside him. "Sorry, Billy. Search engine didn't work. But we met a lot of interesting people."

"What's that?" Carol yelled. "What'd I hear? Next thing Sam will be hanging around the mall, wearing rollerblades, talking to girls."

Sam winked at Billy. "The Dreadful Sister speaks. What does she know, eh?" He got up and raised both arms like he had when they were dancing. He lifted one foot over the other. He'd use Yahoo for a search for lesnoto and maybe for folk dancing.

Billy had fallen asleep. Sam closed the door.

Somewhere, Sam thought to himself, there was an answer. There were always answers if you just asked the right question, if you just learned where to ask. If you got the Boolian phrases right. The man in the pink turban said there was an answer. They'd just have to keep looking, and if they looked, they would find something. Not necessarily what they expected, but something interesting. Science, he said, was good, but magic was good, too.

"Xplthgrdkja," Sam tried to say. His tongue tripped over it. But he was getting closer. When Billy said it tomorrow, he'd listen more carefully. Try to hear exactly what he was trying to say.

THE SAND ARTIST

"I need brushes and paper and paints," Rainbow said.

"Haven't got any," her mother replied. She was busy weaving baskets out of bull kelp and decorating them with moss.

"I'm going to be an artist."

"Good," her mother said.

"To be an artist, I need brushes and paper and paints," Rainbow explained. "Watercolors."

"The markets haven't started," her mother said.

Rainbow knew what that meant. The Christmas season markets hadn't started yet. Her mother had spent all fall weaving baskets and wreaths, getting ready for the weekends in church basements and school gymnasiums. That's when the crafts people set up tables and sold their jams and jellies and weaving and woodcraft and pottery and farm goods to city people who, instead of living in shacks on the beach, crowded together in apartment blocks and condominiums.

Rainbow only vaguely remembered living in the city in a house. That was when she still had a dad. After he left, they'd lived in an apartment. Her mother was always telling her to be quiet so as not to disturb the neighbors, and she had to wear a key around her neck. None of the shacks on the beach had locks, so nobody needed keys.

Sometimes, when things went wrong and her mom went on a rant, Rainbow worried that she'd have to go back to living in an apartment and going to school instead of studying at home. She'd have to take buses and watch TV instead of beach-combing and picking salal and gathering moss and seaweed.

"Brushes and paints and paper don't cost much,"

Rainbow replied. "If we..." But her mother waved a piece of seaweed at her.

"Be creative," she said. "Seek and ye shall find. Be one with the universe."

When her mother started talking like that, Rainbow knew it was no use arguing. Still, having a mother who was one with the universe and wore flowers in her hair was better than having one who worked overtime and microwaved TV dinners.

Rainbow retreated to Joe's. He'd appeared on the beach one day carrying a big packsack and a sleeping bag. They thought he was just one of those day trippers who'd stay for a night or two and then disappear again. Instead, he got out a short, collapsible shovel like the ones you can buy in an army surplus, dug a pit in the sand and roofed it over with drift logs and a blue plastic tarp. He lived there for a week, cooking his food over an open fire.

One day he started to clear a spot in the bush. They thought he was going to put up a tent. Instead, he disappeared up the trail. He didn't come back until the next day, but when he did he was carrying a bale of hay. He set it down, then disappeared up the trail again. He returned in a little while with another bale of hay.

"Going to keep a herd of cows," Doreen said. Doreen was Rainbow's best friend. She told fortunes and read tea leaves. "Maybe we'll be able to get fresh milk."

Joe laid the hay bales in a square. Then he piled more bales on top. He left spaces for two windows and a door.

"I'll huff and I'll puff and I'll blow his house down," Doreen said.

"He says," Morning Lily told them, "that it'll be the warmest house on the beach. Thick insulation and no drafts."

"Remember the three little pigs," Doreen replied.

But the walls stayed up. Joe added a shanty roof that he covered with tin. He found a bright-green door and two windows with black frames. He used his own ax and a borrowed hammer and nails to make a table and chairs out of willow and birch. He even made some shelves.

"What next?" Doreen asked.

A week later they saw him digging a long, narrow hole in the sand. He lined it with rocks. Then he went off and came back with a metal bed frame. He put it over the hole. Someone said he was building a barbecue pit. Someone else thought he was going to make some sort of modern art.

The next day Joe and Morning Lily went up the trail together. Someone said they saw them drive off together in his van. A couple of hours later, they reappeared. This time they were carrying a bright-red cast-iron bathtub. They carried it down the beach and set it on the metal bed frame.

"You fill the tub up with sea water," Morning Lily said. "You put wood in the fire pit, light it up, get the water good and hot and have a bath."

"Throw in a carrot and some spuds and you'll make a fine stew," Doreen shot back. Everyone laughed but they kept looking at the tub. None of them had tubs. Some of them hadn't had a bath in a real tub for five years or more. Mostly they bathed in round metal galvanized washtubs. When it was warm enough they washed in the ocean.

"I'm not having a bath in public," Doreen said.

"He's going to get some plywood and put up some walls. We can even put on a roof. Only rule is you've got to haul your own water and wood and you've got to empty 'er when you're finished and scrub 'er out."

"I'd feel like a boiling lobster," Doreen whispered.

"Oh, I can feel it," Rainbow's mom said. "Imagine all stretched out in hot water."

Even Doreen finally used the tub. The tub broke the ice. It was pretty hard not to talk to a man whose tub you were using.

Since Joe was next door, Rainbow started going over to sit and watch him make furniture out of willow. When he wasn't making furniture, he was taking day jobs working for the local farmers, fixing fences or digging ditches.

"I'm going to be an artist," Rainbow said.

"Bankers make more money than artists. You could be a stockbroker or the head of some big company. You could fly around the world on the Concorde and eat caviar."

"I don't like fish eggs."

Joe was making a large chair with a curved back. He was bending the willow into curves and nailing it in place.

"I'm deprived," Rainbow added. "Diminished. Dumbfounded. Deformed. Destroyed." She liked words that started with the same letter. "My career is being delayed. What if van Gogh's mother wouldn't buy him paints?"

"He might not have chopped off his ear."

"Rejected. Refused. Ridiculed. Ruffled."

"Rhinocerosed," Joe added.

"You can't be rhinocerosed!"

"If a rhinoceros came thundering down the beach and ran right over you and we all went to look and there you were trampled into the sand and a city person with a picnic basket came up and said, 'What happened to her?' what would I say? I'd say, 'She was rhinocerosed.'"

Rainbow shook her head. There was no use arguing with him. Someone said that before he'd started traveling, he'd taught at a university. She could believe it. He knew more words than anyone. He even knew words that started with X. No one could beat him at Scrabble.

"Sometimes we need to look around us," Joe said. "Most people wouldn't look at a bunch of willow and see furniture. If you're an artist you've got an imagination."

"Humph!" Rainbow said. There were times that, good friend or not, Joe was impossible.

She walked as far down the beach as she could, hopping from one log to another without putting her foot on the sand. She cupped her hand to her forehead and squinted at the sea. Some days the strangest things washed up on the beach. Not just glass fishing floats from Japan but stuff that was washed off ships during storms. One time it was shoes. Another time it was jogging outfits. Once it was cases of tea. No one had to buy tea for over a year.

If life was fair, she thought, somewhere out at sea, a storm was washing art supplies overboard and sending them to her.

Today, though, the weather was calm. The sea was flat. The tide was out. When the tide was out, the beach was a sheet of sand from point to point.

"Be creative," her mother had said. Annoyed,

Rainbow kicked the sand. No paint, no paper, no brushes. She had nothing to be creative with.

She picked up a stick and jabbed the sand. She dragged the stick behind her. When she turned around to walk backwards, she saw the mark the line had made. She stopped and drew a circle. Then she drew in eyes and nose and a mouth. She drew the long body of a woman in a flowing dress. She found an old metal pail and scavenged different-sized sticks from the beach.

"These," she sniffed when her mother asked about the bucket full of sticks, "are my paint brushes."

She drew dogs and horses and fish and boats and trees and people and unicorns and angels. She hauled bull kelp to make hair for her mermaids and seashells for their scales.

Her pictures became bigger. And bigger. And bigger.

People came to see what she was doing, but when they were too close they could only see part of the picture. So they climbed back up the trail to look down on the beach. Then they could see the cod and the salmon and halibut, the skates and the crabs and the sea serpents.

One day a boy with blond hair and glasses came to watch. He stayed and helped Rainbow for a couple of hours, carrying buckets of shells and stones.

When she came in for supper, her mother said, "I see you've got a boyfriend."

"A city kid," Rainbow said. "His folks were here having a picnic."

"Is he an artist, too?"

"No," Rainbow said. "He knows all about computers. He says that there's a satellite up there somewhere that could take pictures of my art. His name's Sam. He says he'll come to the Moss Street Market when we go there to sell."

"Uh-huh," her mom said.

"Don't say uh-huh like that," Rainbow said. "There's no uh-huh. He's just some city kid who didn't have anything better to do."

"Uh-huh," her mom said.

The next day Rainbow found a long branch with a piece of trunk still attached. It looked like a plow with a single blade. It was perfect for dragging along and creating a rough line in the sand. She used it to draw outlines, then made dresses from purple mussel shells and white clam shells. Joe left his furniture building to help her. Her mother came and the three of them made sand art together.

"You like Joe, don't you," Rainbow said as her mom was chopping up vegetables to make them all a stew.

"He's just a friend."

"Uh-huh," Rainbow said. She noticed that her

mom was wearing her long purple dress that waved softly like seaweed when the tide runs over it.

The crafters owned an old yellow bus. Everyone had chipped in to help pay for it. They used it to buy supplies and to go to the markets. Sometimes, since Joe had come, Rainbow and her mom would use his green van instead of the bus. He'd stack his furniture in it and pile their baskets and wreaths and dried-flower arrangements in and around the furniture.

Then the three of them would crowd into the front seat with Rainbow in the middle and head off to Sooke or Metchosin or Victoria. Joe said it was a great adventure because you never knew what you might see or do. Each time they left the parking lot, they were facing the Great Unexpected. Sometimes the Great Unexpected was that the van broke down.

Now and again, when they went to sell at a fair and stopped for corn on the cob and ice cream, Rainbow wondered if this was what having a father would have been like. Three of them doing things together. Not big things, not like flying on the Concorde or cruising on a big white ship, but little things like skipping stones in the water or stopping to buy fruit at the roadside and eating it and throwing the pits out the window.

She liked wandering around the markets and dancing to the xylophone band. She liked seeing the homemade pottery, the dolls, the wooden toys, the necklaces and earrings, the vegetables and spices, the home-baked bread and pies and preserves. But it left her frazzled.

"Frazzled," she'd say to her mom when they returned home. "I'm frazzled. I've got to go stand on my head until I calm down." She'd go out onto the beach and stand on her head and do cartwheels and run all the way to the south point. If she was maximum frazzled, she'd have to stand on her head six times. By the time she got back she'd be unfrazzled.

At the market there were always street artists who set up their easels and drew their pictures while everyone watched. One of them had a sign saying, "Bob Billy. Street artist. Five dollars per sketch."

Rainbow took a flat board and a pen and made a sign that said, "Rainbow. Beach artist. No charge." She borrowed a hammer and nail from Joe. She nailed the board to a stick and fitted the stick into a hole in one of the large logs that lay on the beach.

"I want," she said to Joe, "to be an artist but I have no supplies. My ambition is being thwarted."

"Crafters can make art from anything."

"No, they can't," she said. "I'm in despair. I'm depressed. I'll have to cut off my ear."

"It's been done," Joe said. "Don't be a copycat."

They went beachcombing. Joe found a string of three wooden corks.

"Art supplies from the sea," he said.

"I don't think so," Rainbow said. "Three corks. Three beat-up, oily, sandy corks."

They took the corks back to Joe's. He got out his pocket knife. He carved one cork into a penguin, another one into a fish. "We'll have to think of something for the third one when I get back," he said. "I've got a gig in Chilliwack. I hear they need primitive furniture to contrast with their wall-to-wall carpet."

Rainbow helped him carry his supplies to the van. When it was packed, he said, "If anyone is selling fudge, I'll bring you some. See you in three days."

On the third day, her mom kept a lookout for Joe. Not that she was obvious or anything. But she'd made his favorite vegetarian lasagna and every so often she'd find some excuse for going out to take a look at the trail. Rainbow walked to the parking lot three times. He didn't come back that day, or the next day or the next.

"I don't like it," her mom said to Doreen.

"Maybe he's just taken off. Some people, when they start driving, just keep going."

"He said he was bringing me fudge," Rainbow said. "Besides, he had to finish carving the corks."

Two days later, a Mountie appeared. He talked to her mom for a long time. Then he went away. Her mom walked all the way to the far end of the beach and then back. Rainbow sat on a log and waited for her.

She sat down beside Rainbow. "There's been a car accident," she said. "Joe's in the hospital."

"When's he coming back?" Rainbow asked.

"Maybe never."

"Never?" Rainbow said. "Maybe next spring so he can come to the markets. Maybe next fall when it's time to pick pine mushrooms." Joe had picked pine mushrooms with them the year before. They could buy groceries for a whole year if they found a good crop of pine mushrooms.

"Rainbow," her mother said, "he got really badly hurt. A semi-trailer went through a stop sign and hit his van. He could die."

"He could come and stay here and we could look after him," Rainbow said.

"No," her mother said. "If he doesn't die, then they're going to send him on an airplane to Ontario. That's where his family lives. They're going to take care of him. He's going to need a special bed and all sorts of things that we don't have."

"Never?" Rainbow said. "Not ever and ever?"

"We'll have to wait and see," her mom said.

Rainbow went outside. It was a gray day. Fog had settled over the water. Rainbow sat first on one log, then another. She went to Joe's shack.

"People come and people go," she said out loud. She'd seen lots of people come to the beach. They always said they were staying but they hardly ever did.

She went and sat on the front step but it didn't feel the same way as when Joe was there making furniture. She didn't know what to do. She tried a few headstands and back flips.

"Do you feel frazzled?" her mother asked.

"Yes. No. I don't know." She thought about it. "No, I don't feel frazzled. I feel discombobulated." She bit her lip. She'd learned discombobulated from Joe.

Finally, she got her bucket full of brushes and went out onto the flat sand.

She began to draw. She drew a starfish, then a crab. Then she began to draw Joe. She drew his long hair and his beard and his vest. She went and collected brightly colored leaves to make his vest. She drew his pants and even his sandals. By the time she had finished, the tide was turning.

Her mother came out. She put her arm around Rainbow.

"Why," she asked, "do you spend all day drawing pictures when the tide just washes them away? It's a lot of work and then there's nothing."

The tide was spreading over Joe's sandals. It was creeping in silently. Spreading out with a fine white line of foam to mark its edge.

"It's not for nothing. I've got them in the art gallery in my mind," Rainbow said. "As long as I remember them they're not really gone."

It was a hard winter. Rainbow's mother nearly broke her leg hiking down the steep trail from the parking lot. There was snow all through Christmas.

Doreen read tea leaves nearly every night, but she never predicted the park warden who turned up and handed everyone official-looking envelopes.

"What's it say?" Rainbow asked.

"The government wants us to move," her mom replied. "They've made this a park. And they don't want anyone living here. Anything left here after March is going to be treated as abandoned and will be dismantled and burned."

"But we're not hurting anyone. We keep the beach clean. That's not fair."

Everyone's face drooped. Their shoulders drooped. They couldn't understand why the government would force them out of their homes. They walked like they were carrying two buckets of sand. Rainbow's mom was still hobbling around. She couldn't put much weight on her leg.

They fought the eviction notices in the press. There were a lot of articles and pictures. The government didn't want pictures in the paper of people's homes being torn down and homeless little children crying. The government people made grumpy noises but they quit coming around. Rainbow cheered up. She'd been prepared to chain herself to a tree and to let anyone who wanted take a picture of her.

She'd just stopped being frazzled when her mother surprised her by saying, "I think it's time to grow up and be sensible."

Rainbow's heart stopped when she heard this. She knew what her mother meant when she said grow up and be sensible. She meant moving back to the city and getting her old job back working for the government.

"Not me," Rainbow said. "I'm never growing up and being sensible."

"Me, neither," said Doreen. "Imagine wearing shoes instead of sandals. Imagine having to wear pantyhose."

"We'll get a real house," her mother said.

"What's wrong with this house?" Rainbow asked. She loved their house. She'd helped scavenge the drift logs that were used for the pillars. She'd helped salvage the barn boards. Her job had been to take all the old nails out of the planks. She and her mother had hiked up and down the highway collecting pop cans, then sat on the beach cutting the ends out, snipping them across and flattening them out to make shingles. She'd got a blister from the tin snips.

When they had enough shingles, the community held a shingling bee and nailed the tins onto the plank roof in overlapping rows. On a sunny day, their roof sparkled.

"I won't go," Rainbow said. "I'll stay with Doreen. I'll live in Joe's cabin. I don't need you to take care of me any more. I can cook and I can wash clothes." Rainbow stamped one foot on the floor, then the other. "There is nothing, I mean nothing, that is going to get me to move. You make me move and I'll run away from home and hitchhike back here." She knew her mother was terrified of her hitchhiking. She had to listen to a lecture about hitchhiking at least once a month.

"We'll talk about it later," her mother said.

Rainbow knew what her mother's we'll-talk-about-it meant. It meant they'd keep talking and talking until her ears surrendered.

In any case they were too busy to argue. It was the first day of the Moss Street Market. Normally, Rainbow looked forward to Moss Street. The market was set up on a schoolyard. The street had a lot of old houses and flowering trees on it. The people who lived in the neighborhood were into saving whales and not eating meat and riding bicycles to work. City granolas, Doreen called them. Weekend hippies with credit cards. The best kind when you had something to sell.

Rainbow hadn't been to the city for months. The houses were all jammed together and the cars raced by. She felt her hair. She could always tell when she started to frazzle because the ends of her hair started to stick out. On a bad day she looked like she'd grabbed an electric fence.

When they reached the market some crafters were already set up. The brightly colored tents and the pennants made Rainbow think of medieval knights and tournaments. Flowered tents, green tents, red tents, blue tents. There was Mary with her famous breads filled with spices and strange-sounding grains. There was the lady with airplanes made from soft-drink cans. Suspended from strings, they spun and swayed in the breeze. The farmers were there selling their bedding plants and early vegetables from the backs of their trucks. There were potters and doll makers and birdhouse builders and wooden toy crafters.

"It wouldn't be so bad," her mom said. "The art gallery is just at the top of the street. They give art lessons. The ocean's at the other end of the street."

"I know where the ocean is," Rainbow said. She'd walked down to the ocean on slow days. There were big cliffs and a parking lot on Clover Point but no proper beaches. There were people walking their dogs and rollerblading and strolling along and kite-flying.

"Most kids love that sort of thing," her mother said.

"Look at my hair," Rainbow replied. "It's sticking straight out. It won't calm down until I get home and stand on my head for five minutes."

The market was so busy that they didn't have time to argue any more. When it finally slowed down, the calypso band was ready to play. Rainbow went over and joined the group that had started to dance. They were dancing all together when she noticed a blond boy around her age dancing beside her.

"Hi!" he yelled over the music. "How's the sand art coming?"

She took a closer look at him. She didn't remember seeing him at any of the craft fairs.

"I helped you make one of your pictures. I carried shells for you."

He was taller, skinnier, but she remembered the glasses. He'd got his hair cut differently. It was nearly shaved around the bottom of his head. She couldn't remember his name.

When the music stopped, he laughed and said, "I'm Sam. I said I'd come to Moss Street."

"I remember," she said. "You know everything about computers and satellites and stuff."

He bought a Coke and put in two straws. He took a sip, then handed her the can.

"You still making art?" he asked.

"Sometimes. You still doing stuff with computers?"

"Home pages. I can do the technicals, but I'm not very good at the art part of it. You want to see the kind of stuff I do? I'm sort of looking for an artist to do the visuals."

"Can't," Rainbow said nervously. "I've gotta work, then we're going back home. I don't know anything about computers. Like I've seen them in the store." She was starting to feel frazzled. Pretty soon her hair was going to lift off. "I don't even know how to turn them on."

"I can show you," Sam said.

Rainbow handed him back his pop. "My mom needs a break so she can get some falafel."

"Who's the friend?" her mom asked.

"Nobody," Rainbow said.

"He looks familiar."

"He's just hanging around the market."

"Somebody, nobody," her mom said, staring in Sam's direction. "What's his name?"

"I don't remember."

"You're getting old. Alzheimer's. We'll have to get you a cane."

"Sam," Rainbow said.

Her mother snapped her fingers. "Sam, the computer man! That's it!"

"Mom! Please!"

"Uh-huh."

"Don't uh-huh me," Rainbow said.

"He just accidentally was here?"

"It happens."

"Uh-huh."

"Buy yourself some lunch."

When her mom went to get falafel, Rainbow breathed a sigh of relief. Her mother was quite capable of waving Sam over, asking him everything about himself, telling him all the embarrassing moments of Rainbow's life. Keeping her mother under control was a chore.

"Your mother says you've got a beau," Doreen said.

"I haven't got a beau," Rainbow declared. "What's with you guys?"

"Just if you had a boyfriend in the city, it'd be easier to get you to move, I guess."

"Forget it," Rainbow said. "I'm not going to no regular school. Doreen, you talk to her. You tell her I can live with you. Or I can live by myself and you'll keep an eye on me."

"One day the cops will come and move us out. Maybe not today or tomorrow but it'll happen."

"Don't you love the beach? You said you love getting up in the morning and there's big surf and the waves are rolling in."

"Yeah, but sometimes you've got to let go of something for something else."

"Not me," Rainbow said. She thought maybe she'd go back to the dancing but then six customers came all at once. The crowds always were biggest between noon and two o'clock. She waved at Strawberry for help. Strawberry lived two beaches over.

Strawberry came over and helped with the customers. "My mom's going nuts," Rainbow said. "Bananas. Bonkers."

"All parents are crazy," Strawberry said. "It's what happens when you become a parent."

"Do you think so?" Rainbow asked. "Like, will it happen to us?"

"Yup," Strawberry said. "We'll be normal and then we'll have kids and then we'll be weird."

"My mom wants to become a city granola," Rainbow said.

"Lucky you," Strawberry said.

"I'm not going to be a weekend hippie. Do you want to live in an apartment?"

"Yeah," Strawberry said. "And go to movies, and go to the shopping mall whenever I want, and..."

"I'll trade you," Rainbow said. "My mother for your folks."

"You want me to live with your mother?"

"What's wrong with my mother? She's not so bad. I mean, she meditates and stuff but she's a pretty good cook, except for her hang-up on tofu."

"I hate tofu."

"You don't have to eat it. Just get her talking about the ozone layer or clear-cutting or something. When she goes out of the room to get some statistics, put the tofu back in the wok."

Rainbow's mother appeared just then with falafel wrapped in pita bread and a drink made from grass. She held up the glass for them to see. "Destroys the free radicals," she said.

"Strawberry and me," Rainbow said, "have cut a deal. She wants to live in the city. I want to live on the land, save the environment, be one with the natural universe. We're trading places. A week from now, you won't notice the difference."

"You can still do your schoolwork at home," her mother said.

"By myself?" She was thinking about Joe's cabin and how they had it set up for a school. They all went there and each person who knew a lot about something came and taught them. They knew more about beach creatures and plants and animals than most people who'd been to university. That's what Harry said. Harry had been a biologist before he dropped out. He was always having them drag something out of the ocean to study or leading them through the bush collecting leaves and snails and bugs.

"We'll go camping at the beach on weekends and holidays."

Rainbow could feel she was losing the argument. It felt like when the tide washed in over her paintings in the sand. Nothing would stop it. She had to hold the images in her head so they wouldn't be lost. Like Sam had said to her that day on the beach, even though the tide came in, she could create a virtual art gallery in her head. Then she could access her pictures whenever she wanted.

"Weekends," Rainbow said.

"Something's better than nothing."

"But why?" She didn't want to cry in front of everyone. She turned around and was going to run away. Then she stopped and stared.

Joe was there. Even without his beard, she knew it was him. He was terribly thin but he had on one of his brightly colored vests and his black hat. He was in a wheelchair.

As he pushed his way toward them, Rainbow stood and stared. It really was him. She grabbed her mom's hand.

"He's got a place. It's not very big, but it's got a ramp and he can get in and out. It's not so far from here. He'd like us to live with him."

Joe stopped in front of them.

"I didn't forget." He handed her a small brown paper bag. She knew there was fudge in it. She took it. "It just took a little while." He struggled to get up. "Give me a hand." Rainbow leaned forward, caught his arm and helped him stand. He took a cane from the side of the wheelchair. "It's going to take awhile but I'm going to be okay. Lots of physio, though."

Rainbow turned. The music had stopped. She looked for Sam. The dancers were spreading out in the crowd. Blond hair, she thought. Where's his blond hair? Then she saw him walking toward the entrance. She caught up to him on the sidewalk.

"Maybe I'd like to try that artist in cyberspace stuff."

"Yeah!" Sam said. "Cool."

"I'm moving into town. I'll see you here next week. That okay?"

"Yeah," Sam said, standing there, looking like he wasn't sure what to say next. "You're going to be here?"

"For sure. Selling stuff. Me and my mom. And Joe." She looked across the fence and through the milling people. Joe was back in his wheelchair but he wasn't looking sad. He was laughing with Doreen and her mom.

Maybe, she thought, maybe in the city she wouldn't have to spend so much time taking care of the adults in her life.

"Cyberart's the way to go. Millions of people on the Web. I'm getting some new software."

"Okay," Rainbow said. It was too much. Her hair

was going to be standing straight up if she didn't get somewhere she could do some somersaults.

She started to walk toward the ocean. Cyberart, she thought, instead of watercolors. It was going to be hard. She kept wanting to cry when she thought about not having the beach any more. Not waking up to the surf and the barking of the seals. But it couldn't be harder than Joe learning to walk again.

Her whole head felt like it was going to lift off. Frazzled, she thought. I'm ultimately frazzled.

She was so busy thinking that she wasn't watching where she was going. She bumped into a guy.

"Sorry," she said.

"It's okay," he replied. He raised two fingers in a V. "Live long and prosper."

She laughed. "Yeah," she said. "Live long and prosper." She could see the ocean from where she was standing. She laughed again. It wasn't like it was going anywhere. It'd still be there when she needed it.

GARBAGE CREEK

Not wanted. That's what Jim was thinking as he kicked a can down the road. With every kick it went spinning away.

Not wanted. Not any more. Now all they could talk about was the baby this and the baby that.

His mom was always saying, "I'm too tired to read to you. Don't make so much noise. Go play quietly." The baby always needed her diapers changed. She was always eating. If she didn't eat so much, she wouldn't need her diapers changed so often.

Jim gave the can another kick. It went flying through the air, off the trail, down the slope and into the creek. He ran down after it. Stupid can, he thought.

He was surprised to see a girl sitting on a rock. He really didn't want to talk to anyone but she was holding the tin can.

"This yours?" she asked.

"Yeah," he said, taking it.

"I'm Angie. I live up there."

"Jim." He pointed back along the creek. "What're you doing?"

"Looking for arrowheads."

He looked around. It was just a little creek with a bunch of junk dumped into it. He sat down on an old tire.

"You want to go to the salt chuck?" Angie asked.

They followed the stream, hopping from rock to rock, wading in the water sometimes. The trees hung over the stream on both sides. They startled a couple of dippers that were looking for insects in the gravel bottom. When they got to the salt chuck, there was a field of grass. There were wild rose bushes and blackberry brambles. They stopped to pick blackberries. They saw a crane and some mallards.

"There used to be salmon in this creek," Angie said on the way back.

"This little thing?"

They searched for arrowheads but didn't find any. Instead they found some tin cans and bottles and plastic. They kept the drink cans and bottles and threw the rest of the garbage onto the bank.

"You're sure there's arrowheads here?" Jim said.

"I've got six at home. Two aren't so good but I've got four good ones. One's red and two are white and one is blue. There's supposed to be a midden but I haven't been able to find it."

That night the baby cried all night. It didn't fall asleep until morning. Jim made himself a peanut butter and jelly sandwich for breakfast. Then his mother chased him outside because she didn't want the baby wakened up.

"You came back," Angie said when he arrived at the creek. "I thought you said there was no point looking for arrowheads here."

"You got any brothers or sisters?"

"Four. They've all moved out. They're too busy to do anything with me."

"I'll give you my sister." Jim had brought a garden trowel. They used it to dig in the gravel and along the bank. They found clam and mussel shells. They found an animal bone that was broken on one end. Angie said that meant someone had dug out the marrow.

As they searched, they kept picking up garbage and tossing it onto the bank.

"No wonder the salmon don't come here any more. I wouldn't, either," Jim said disgustedly. "Look at this." It was the rusted front wheel of a bicycle. He heaved it out of the water. "They call this Sugar Creek. I think they should call it Garbage Creek."

"How come you spend your time down here?"

"There's no place at home for me. How about you?"

"No reason. Just there's never anyone there. Me and the TV."

Jim picked up a plastic grocery bag. He started putting bits of junk in it. "You really think the Indians used to camp here? I looked up midden in the dictionary."

"My dad said my grandpa's dad used to come here in the fall to spear salmon. They'd come down in their canoes and set up camp. It's not Indians. It's Cowichan. My dad's Cowichan."

They wrestled part of an old fridge out of the water.

"You know," Jim said. "About the salmon. Do you think, I mean, if you and me got rid of the junk..."

Angie sat down on a rock. "I've been wanting to try but there's just been me and I can't move some of the big things. Two can do a lot more than one."

After that, they met every day at the stream. Every day they pulled out garbage and raked over the gravel. Sometimes they found things people had thrown into the water the night before. Jim made signs saying "No littering" and nailed them up on some sticks.

"How's your sister doing?" Angie asked one afternoon.

"Noisy. She's always crying. My mom's always changing her diapers and giving her a bottle. She wakes them up at night and then they're grouchy in the morning. What about your parents?"

"Working. My dad's a carver and he's always going places to show his carving. My mom works for the government."

They met nearly every day for the rest of the summer. They made a trip on their bikes out to the Salmon House and watched all the movies and studied all the displays. They took the bus to the library and read books on salmon. They borrowed their parents' shovels and rakes. They saw belted kingfishers. One day they counted six eagles. As they were cleaning up the creek, they saw crayfish and diving beetles.

"Those are called water tigers," Jim said, showing Angie a diving-beetle larva.

They were still looking for arrowheads. They found some chipped flakes of rock and a stone that might have been used as a hammer. They took a couple of days off to go to Totem Pole Park and the provincial museum. They looked at the masks and sat in the longhouse.

"My dad makes masks like that," Angie said. "And pictures and stuff."

"My dad has a computer business. People are always calling with problems."

"I'm Cowichan and Scots. What about you?"

"Canadian."

"Me, too. But the other stuff. Before you got here."

"Ukrainian. Polish. My dad says my mom is the peroghi princess."

On one of their trips to the library, they stopped at the Ukrainian center and Jim showed Angie some books written in Ukrainian. "Crazy alphabet, eh?" They went downstairs and watched some dancers practicing for a concert.

"Can you talk Ukrainian?"

Jim counted on his fingers. "Six words. Can you talk Cowichan?"

Angie counted on her fingers. "Eight."

"I'll teach you six Ukrainian words if you teach me eight Cowichan."

They went back to their stream. They kept hauling out junk and raking over the gravel to get rid of the clay someone had dumped. One day they hiked to a second larger creek. It was too big and deep to cross. They stood on the bank looking at it. It was clogged with debris from logging. Garbage was caught among the branches and small logs.

"I looked this one up," Jim said. "It's called Washing Creek. It used to have salmon, too. Lots of them."

September came and it was time to go back to school. They visited their stream on weekends. But Jim had a job delivering flyers and Angie was involved in sports so they weren't able to make it every weekend.

"Hey, guy," his dad said one day. "What's so interesting about the sky? You keep looking up all the time, you'll get a crick in your neck."

"Rain clouds," Jim said. He was thinking about how the salmon would be returning soon and they needed water.

The baby had an ear infection. She'd been crying for days. That meant a trip to the doctor. Then they all went shopping for a crib. When they came out of the mall, it was raining.

After that it rained pretty regularly. On the last weekend in October, Jim met Angie at the bus stop and they took the bus out to Goldstream Park. The salmon were running. The parking lot was jammed. There were people lined up all along the river bank. Clouds of seagulls filled the air. Maple leaves as big as plates were twirling to the ground.

They walked along the river bank. They could see the backs of the chum sticking out of the water. There were lots of them. Here and there were the cherry-red backs of the coho.

"It's too crowded," Jim said.

They took the bus back. Neither one said much. They were thinking about Garbage Creek. About all the work they had done. They walked to the stream, sort of hurrying, then slowing down, like they wanted to get there but they didn't want to get there.

The rain was coming down steadily. There was a foot of water in the stream. They walked along the bank.

"No more fish than arrowheads," Jim said disgustedly.

"Maybe it's been too long. Maybe the fish forgot there's a stream here."

"Maybe we need to do a salmon dance."

"Don't know one."

The next day Angie took two bags out of her packsack. Carefully, she unfolded tissue paper. First she took out one mask, then another. They were carved from cedar and were painted in bright colors. One was a salmon mask. The other was of a beaver.

"These are mine," she said. "I've got eagle and killer whale, too, but I thought they'd frighten the salmon. Maybe if we wear these, the fish will remember. Maybe the stream will look like it did a long time ago."

They went to where the stream and the salt marsh met. They sat side by side in the tall grass and held the masks over their faces.

Suddenly, Angie grabbed Jim's arm. She put her finger to her lips, then pointed.

There, just inside the entrance, hiding under the overhanging bank, were two coho, their tails slowly moving back and forth. Cautiously, the fish edged into the stream. They moved forward, then let the current push them back. In a sudden burst the female made a dash forward. The male followed. Then the female stopped, turned on her side and began to beat the gravel violently with her tail.

"She's making a redd," Jim whispered excitedly.

The female kept beating at the gravel until there was a small depression. She tested the depth with her tail. She lay over it and they could see her laying the eggs. Then the male swam forward to fertilize the eggs. The female rushed ahead and began to make a new nest.

Angie and Jim watched for hours. The female's

tail gradually became tattered. Both fish lay still in the current.

"They're tired," Angie said. "All that work to make a nest and have some babies."

Angie and Jim came back to the stream the next day and the next. Gradually, the two fish became covered in white blotches. On the third day, both fish were floating in an eddy.

"It's not fair," Angie said.

"No." Jim was sitting on a rock. He'd got so he thought of the two salmon as his salmon. "Lots of things aren't fair. They just are."

During the winter, because they went to different schools and were busy with homework and sports and clubs, they only got to meet at the creek occasionally. The trees had shed their leaves. The water looked cold.

One Friday Jim called Angie and asked her to meet him at the creek. He felt sort of shy. They hadn't seen each other for awhile. They both said hello. They asked each other about school.

"How're things going at home?" Angie asked.

"Okay, I guess. She's crawling around and she can just about say something. She wants to climb on top of me when I'm lying on the floor watching TV. I'm helping her learn to walk. How about you?"

"My oldest brother took me to a rock concert in Vancouver."

"The eggs should be hatching now," Jim said. "I wrote it on my calendar." He took out a pamphlet he had got on salmon. They searched but couldn't find anything.

"They're too little," Angie said. "They're still alevins. They're hiding under the gravel. We've got to wait until April."

Jim checked the creek every couple of weeks. He saw a mink and a deer and a number of cranes but no salmon fry. Then, the first week in April, Angie called him. They met at the creek on a Saturday morning.

They were standing in the water, peering down. All at once, Jim shouted, "Look! There they are."

Salmon fry scattered through the water.

Jim laughed. "We're parents." He felt embarrassed. "I mean...you know what I mean."

"Grandparents. Next year we'll be great-grandparents."

There weren't a lot of fry. But there were some. Jim and Angie looked up and down the stream. Someone had thrown some paper cups into it in spite of the signs. They picked them up and put them in a garbage bag.

They crouched down to watch the fry dart about.

"Ours," Angie said. "We did it. They wouldn't be here if it weren't for us."

Jim nodded and grinned. "We never found any arrowheads though."

Angie reached into her pocket. "Put your hand out," she said. "I brought you something." She took her hand out of her pocket, then held it over his. She put something in his hand. It was her blue arrowhead.

He put his hand in his pocket. He took out a wooden doll. He turned the top. It came apart. Inside was another little doll. He opened this one and there was another doll inside. "I brought you something, too," he said and gave it to her. "To celebrate."

They both looked at the water. Here and there they could see the fry darting back and forth.

"We've still got work to do," Angie said. "They're going to be here for a year before they go to sea. You and me, we're going to have keep Sugar Creek clean for them. And maybe even another pair will turn up in the fall."

"Being a parent is hard work," Jim said, laughing. He looked at Angie. Maybe, he thought, if his sister turned out like Angie, it wouldn't be so bad having her around after all.